For Dominique
Just because

$\mathcal{J}$ohn Lennon was named John Lennon after John Lennon.

But everyone called him Beatle.

Beatle was eighteen years old, born on the eighteenth of December.

His twin sister, Winsome, was also eighteen years old, born six weeks later and in an entirely different year on the first of February.

Nonidentical twins with nonidentical birthdays.

As you can imagine, their births had been very big news at the time. They scored front page of the newspaper, as well as an entry in the *Guinness World Records* book under the category "Longest Interval Between Twins"; a title they held for a couple of years before another set of twins trumped them with a massive eighty-four days between the first and second.

Here's a science class for you: if Beatle and Winsome had been monozygote twins, separate birthdays in separate months would have been impossible. Monozygote twins come from a split egg, which means they share the same amniotic sac and placenta—so if one is born, both are outta there. But Beatle and Winsome were dyzygotes. Two eggs with separate placentas, separate amniotic cavities.

Separate birthdays.

And separate star signs.

Eighteen years ago on the eighteenth of December, when the twins were twenty-nine weeks in the womb (a normal pregnancy is forty weeks), their mom had collided with an oncoming car.

And promptly gone into labor.

So had the other driver, just about.

Their mom was rushed to the hospital in Melbourne, where it was discovered that the water of one twin's sac—Beatle's—had broken during the accident, and he was heading out into the big wide world, like it or not. The other twin's sac—Winsome's—was as it should be, so she was able to stay tucked up inside her mom, monitored carefully, for six more weeks.

Every morning and every afternoon the nurses had wheeled their mom down from her hospital bed on the third floor—where she was lying quietly, keeping Winsome safe inside the womb—down to the intensive care unit on the first floor, where Beatle lay inside an incubator with: a sock on his head to keep him warm;

pads and wires stuck all over his body to monitor his vital signs; a tube down his throat to feed food straight into his stomach and another tube up his nose giving him oxygen.

"You were like a little skinned rabbit," Beatle's mom was fond of telling him. As if a skinned rabbit was something cute and endearing, instead of something hideous and gruesome and disgusting.

The front page headline of the paper on the third of February read, "The Lennons: something to sing about," with a photo of Winsome cuddled up in the crook of their mom's arm and one of Beatle lying in the incubator looking—to be honest—like something your mom would buy from the local butcher. He had these twig-like arms and legs, and his skin was shiny and sticky as if he were a burn victim, and he had tubes sticking up his nose, and you know how babies are all soft and sweet and adorable? Well, he wasn't.

As Beatle had gotten older, he'd gotten used to the same questions in the same order:

"So your sister has her birthday six weeks later than you?"

"Yeah."

"And you're born in different months?"

"Yuh."

"And different years?"

"Uh huh."

"But you're twins?"

"Right."

"But isn't that weird?"

And Beatle would shrug.

"Well," he'd say, "it's just the same as anyone else. *You* don't have *your* birthday on the same day as your brother or sister, do you?"

"But it's not the same. You're twins."

And then they'd go on:

"Do you know what each other is thinking?"

"Can you feel each other's pain?"

"Have you ever had any psychic experiences?"

And on:

"Do you have a day in the middle that you both celebrate on?"

"Does she feel like your birthday is hers?"

"Do you feel like her birthday is yours?"

And on:

"Do you feel like you should have been born in February?"

"Do you think you're more a Sagittarius or an Aquarius type person?"

This last question—the Sagittarius vs. Aquarius question—always bugged Beatle, because, to be honest, he wondered the same thing himself.

This was quite likely due to the fact that every morning

his mom read out two horoscopes for him: Sagittarius and Aquarius. The date he was born, and the date he was meant to be born.

"Okay, Beatle," she'd say, patting the newspaper flat onto the table, her rings knocking against the wood. "Sagittarius says 'The Full Moon in the middle of this month brings issues to a peak. It's time for a change.'"

And Beatle would squint his eyes—just a bit, just enough to make it convincing, as if he were committing to memory the fact that the Full Moon was going to bring changes—then nod his head and get back to shovelling Cheerios into his mouth.

"And Aquarius says," his mom would continue, and chuck her chin in Winsome's direction, "this is for you, too, not just Beatle," and Winsome would raise her eyes as if she couldn't give a shit, which she couldn't, "'. . . Venus enters your House until June. This rare astro-passage means love is going to come from surprising directions.'"

And Winsome would sigh dramatically to get the message across to their mom that it was so BORRRRING to have to listen to this crap every morning, and Beatle would say, "Venus, gotcha," then get back to his breakfast. Because whether or not Venus was in his House, his Cheerios were in his breakfast bowl and they had to take priority.

This is probably as good a point as any to mention

that it wasn't just horoscopes that did Beatle's head in. He was also shamefacedly superstitious.

Black cats, ladders, broken mirrors, umbrellas open inside? Terrified of them all. As for Friday the 13th, Beatle happened to know (he'd read it on the Internet) that the *British Medical Journal* had published a study of Friday the 13th which showed that fifty-two percent more people were admitted to the hospital from car accidents on Friday the 13th than on Friday the sixth. And that's a fact. Scientifically proven. *British Medical Journal*, if you don't mind.

He'd also read on the Internet that if thirteen people sit down for dinner at a table on a Friday, within a year one of those people will be dead. Not a fact, necessarily—and certainly not verified by the *British Medical Journal*—but a superstition that a person wouldn't want to be testing willy-nilly.

Today was Friday the 13th of February, the first Friday the 13th of the year. Beatle had two more to live through before the year was out: Friday the 13th of March and Friday the 13th of November. On this particular Friday the 13th, Beatle had been down at the Espy Hotel playing pool with Toby and Magnus, but just after nine he'd turned into a pumpkin and left to catch the tram home. Because, while he was happy to get out and about and not let his superstitions rule his life, he figured it didn't pay to push that fifty-two-percent statistic too far.

At the tram stop just down the road, he saw a girl sitting under the shelter, reading a book, wearing her sunglasses. At nine o'clock at night. When the sun's tucked up in bed. Sure, in other parts of the world there might still be a need for your shades at nine o'clock in the p.m., but in Melbourne-Australia-the-Southern-Hemisphere, the need for sunglasses is well and truly done and dusted by that time of night.

Beatle grinned as he plonked down on the seat beside her.

"Your future's so bright, eh?" he said.

She looked over and studied him, not saying anything, as if trying to decide whether he was a creep, a pervert, or your regular, creeps-giving sleaze. And then she sighed as if it were all too tiresome.

"God, don't you start," she said, pushing her hair behind her ear.

Beatle leaned back against the shelter and folded his arms across his chest, rejigging himself subconsciously to make sure he looked every bit as good as she did. Because she sure looked good. Spanish, or something, with a strong, straight nose and an over-large mouth, and when she spoke you expected an accent, but there was no accent. Instead, there was a lisp. Or not really a lisp, but a slight sibilant *sss*omething underlining each of her words. As if her tongue were a fraction too big for her mouth.

"The night I've had." She spread her fingers like a rising sun in order to better catalog her dramas. "First," she said, hitting her pointer finger, "I had a Friday detention for something so pathetic I won't even bore you with the details. Then," she hit her middle finger, "I had no credit left in my phone so I couldn't call my friends. Then," she hit her ring finger, "Mathilde *finally* called," with a big, breathy emphasis on "finally," "but I was at home by then, and my mom had a few things she wanted me to do before I went out. Basically, she was punishing me for the detention I got, which seems pretty unfair—seeing as a detention is punishment in itself, so to punish someone for being punished probably goes against the Geneva Convention or something—anyway, so that's why I didn't end up meeting Tild and everyone until seven, but by the time I got there," she hit her pinky finger, "they'd organized tickets to see Blue Train—how awesome would that be; they're playing at the Prince tonight—but because they didn't know if I was coming down or not, they didn't get me a ticket, which is why they're off seeing the band now, and I'm on my way home on a Friday night at nine o'clock. And then," she switched hands because she'd run out of fingers, "I left my glasses in Tild's handbag—long story—so now I have to wear my sunglasses to read my book and I'll tell you something for free, there's definitely something to be said for Friday the thirteenth, because mine's been totally shitful. How about yours?"

Beatle stared at her for a moment.

"You wanna go get an ice cream?" he asked.

She raised her sunglasses and put them on top of her head, then looked at him more closely. Her eyes were large and brown with these massively long eyelashes that dusted her cheeks each time she blinked as their contribution to the natural housekeeping of the world. The way she looked at him made him feel as if she were looking way inside him, digging right down, and caused him to physically squirm in the seat beside her.

"An ice cream?" she said.

"You know." He shrugged. "Make your day a little less shitful."

She narrowed her eyes at him and pushed her mouth out.

"Could be good," she said slowly, looking at him a bit more carefully. "But what if you're a psychopath?"

Beatle stared at her for another moment, then nodded.

"That," he said, thinking it through, "would explain my bizarre appetite for human flesh and sacrificial virgins."

She grinned at him and raised an eyebrow.

"Well, if you're after a sacrificial virgin, I'm not your

girl," she said, tilting her chin so that her neck looked long and lean and good enough to sink your teeth into.

"Don't fit the criteria, eh?" Beatle said, his eyes opening wide.

"Excuse me," she said, crossing her leg and looking like a librarian who is very prim and proper and somehow makes you think of sex more than those obvious girls who . . . okay, they make you think of sex, too. "I just meant—virgin or not—I don't want to be sacrificed."

"Virgin or not?"

"You know what I mean." She pushed her hair off her face as if that would help untangle the mess she was now in. "I'm not interested in having you eat me."

Beatle burst out laughing.

Both her hands slapped up to her mouth, trying to tuck the words back inside.

"I didn't mean it like that," she continued breathlessly. "I meant, you know, eating, as in gorging on my human flesh. The thing is," she shook her head, "you're the one who started it with all this talk about human flesh and sacrificial virgins and everything." She put on a serious face. "I don't usually chat with strangers about . . ."

Beatle's mouth tried to contain the thoughts that were bouncing against the inside of his cheeks.

"Oral sex?" he suggested.

"Omigod," she said, smacking his arm. "No! That wasn't what I was going to say."

"Just trying to be helpful," he said, rubbing where she'd hit him.

He stood up and held out his hand in the first act of chivalry he'd managed to rustle up since he'd met her five minutes ago.

"Ice cream?" he said.

She looked up at him—the whites of her eyes even bigger and whiter and more appealing from that angle—then offered her hand delicately, like some kind of damsel in distress. Although Beatle couldn't see much evidence of distress.

"Might as well get it over and done with." She sighed, and then crossed the road to where the bright lights beckoned, without even checking first for traffic.

*T*he Morton Lane Bar is a dark little bar in a back street behind the Espy Hotel. Not many people know about it; in fact Beatle isn't even sure it's legal. You go up to this normal-looking house, ring the doorbell, and wait until someone comes to let you in. No password or secret sign or handshake, none of that sort of thing, although there should be. It's that kind of place. Dark and espionage-y. The sort of joint where you expect a shaved-headed, bull-necked type of guy to slide back a little letterbox-sized slot in the door and check you out before deciding if you can or can't come in. But instead, a girl with pierced lips opens the door and steps back to let you pass. Never asks you for ID, just opens the door and in you go. Inside it's small and poky and dark and hazy from smoke and lots of people standing around talking, and there's no music, but lots of noise anyway.

Beatle hadn't intended to come here. He'd planned on getting an ice cream, eating it, then catching the tram home. No matter how pretty she was, and no matter how insanely big her lips were, he hadn't planned on being out late on Friday the 13th. Not with that fifty-two percent statistic hanging over his head. But they'd had their ice creams, and she'd asked him what had happened to his foot—why he was limping—and he'd told her it was kind of a long story, so she'd suggested maybe they should go get a drink somewhere so he could tell her all about it. And Beatle thought there couldn't possibly be any harm in that, especially seeing as the Morton Lane Bar was just around the corner. So now here he was, sitting in a bar on Friday the 13th next to Destiny—that was her name, Destiny—watching her swizzle her drink with a straw.

"All the kids in my family have names that 'mean' something," she was saying, putting her hands up on either side of her face and jabbing her fingers down quickly, twice, to make quote marks. "First there's Grace. She's the oldest. Then Prudence, Patience, Frank, Faith, Charity, Hope, me. I get the hippy, trippy name." She rose her eyes to the heavens. "And then Ernest."

Beatle grinned.

"Ernest?"

"Yep. And if you think I'm not happy about my name, don't ever get him started on his."

She shook her head.

"Apparently it was either that or Victor," she said,

pushing her hair back behind her ear again. "You see," and she wagged her finger at him, "that's the problem with going themed names and then having lots of kids. You run out of choices by the end, and we get stuck—you know, me and Ern—with the crap names."

"My sister's name's Winsome," Beatle said. "They could have called you that."

"What's that mean?"

"You know, charming, winning, that type of thing."

"And is she?"

"No."

Destiny grinned, swizzling her drink as she rested her elbow on the table, her wrist making a delicate, upside-down U.

"Okay, so your sister's Winsome," she said, looking up at him through her lashes, "even though she isn't. Where does Beatle come from? It's not your real name?"

"No. My real name's John Lennon. As in The Beatles." And he opened his hands in a shrug, as if that explained everything.

Destiny stopped swizzling.

"No way," she said, smiling at him as if they were related. Which Beatle seriously hoped they weren't— not with the thoughts that were starting to swizzle around inside his head. "That's weird," she continued. "I'm Destiny McCartney. As in Paul McCartney and The

Beatles. Snap," and she smacked her hand down on the table.

Beatle stared at her. For a guy with a distorted sense of superstitions and signs, this was quite a coincidence. Then something tickled at his brain, nudging at him like a dog nosing his elbow.

"Hang on a sec," he said, pointing his finger at her. "You said you had a brother, Frank?"

She nodded.

"He doesn't teach English?" Beatle continued.

Destiny grinned at him.

"Twelfth grade," she said, nodding. "Elwood High."

"He's my teacher," Beatle said, shaking his head.

"No way."

"Yes way."

"Well," Destiny said, going back to swizzling her drink, "I don't know what it was, but you must have done something terrible in a former life to land my brother as your teacher." She toasted him with her drink. "So, Mr. Lennon, on behalf of the McCartneys, pleased to meet you. Maybe we should consider getting the band back together." She slugged back the last of her drink, before plonking her glass down on the table.

Beatle looked at her for a long moment, then drained the last of his glass, too.

"Another?" he asked.

"Sure."

He went up to the bar and came back with two more drinks.

"So," she said, resting her chin on her shoulder in an altogether appealing way, "you limp. Why?"

Beatle looked down at his foot. His stupid foot that he hated. He chewed at his lip, wondering exactly how much to tell her. He could just imagine how she'd react once he told her: like he was some kind of freak.

Everyone knew why he limped. *Everyone*. Even people he didn't know: the man at the newsstand; the lady at the pharmacy; kids at school he'd never spoken to. They all knew him and knew what had happened. And they all felt sorry for him. "Poor Beatle," he'd hear them whispering behind his back. But tonight, here, with Destiny, she didn't know anything. He could tell her whatever he liked.

And he liked the thought of not telling her the truth.

So he said, "It's a long story that involves a shark and some Mafioso type guys in Shanghai over a long, hot summer."

"Really?"

"Yes. I can't say anything more about it, otherwise the government might need to silence you for knowing too much."

"Well, now you've got my attention," she said, putting

her elbow on the table and nibbling thoughtfully on her thumbnail. "Mr. Mysterious."

He winked at her.

"I only just got it now?" he asked.

"Well, yeah. Sharks and Shanghai, I mean, come on. Until then you were a bit of a yawn."

And she bit her bottom lip in a way that Beatle found irresistible.

"Thanks," he said.

"But now; see now you've piqued my interest. When did I start being interesting to you?" she asked.

Beatle grinned.

"Somewhere around the time you mentioned not being a sacrificial virgin and me eating you."

She smacked him on the shoulder.

"Omigod. You know I didn't mean it like that. It's difficult for me to move on if you keep bringing it up every twenty seconds."

And then—Beatle wasn't entirely sure how—their conversation drifted, swirling here and there until they were talking peas.

"You see," Destiny said, sitting close to Beatle. Very close. Close enough for Beatle to notice that his breath seemed to be catching on one of the ribs in his chest, like a plastic bag hooking onto a branch of a tree and unable to free itself. "I really like the taste of peas. But

I can't stand the way they're so small. You know what I mean?"

"Yeah, and you've got to mash them onto the back of your fork," he said, "which is pretty annoying."

"Exactly," she said, having a final swig of her drink, then putting the glass back down on the table. "So I've decided to invent big ones. You know, genetically modified ones. Breed them with pumpkins or something. So that when you want a pea, you just boil up one. Not a squillion of them. And you don't have to squash it, or anything, it's right there, ready to eat."

"But the annoying thing," Beatle pointed out, "would be you'd then have to cut it up in order to make it small enough to fit in your mouth."

"That's true." Destiny frowned. "I hadn't thought of that. That's a bit inconvenient, isn't it?"

"Kind of."

Destiny leaned back against the booth. A smile seemed to be playing around her eyes, but her mouth was straight. Beatle leaned back against the booth, too, close enough to be able to smell her. She smelled kind of flowery. A bit perfumey, but also a bit just-her. Beatle put his hand over hers. She didn't move it away.

"So, that's peas covered," Beatle said, arching an eyebrow. "What about your Q's?"

He intertwined his fingers with hers. Looked at the

contrast between his hand, the big guy fingers, compared with her small-and-pleasantly-delicate-against-his ones.

"Well," Destiny said, biting her lip, "I'm not crazy about them. But seeing as we're talking letters, I like staring into your I's."

And she fluttered her eyelashes at him before collapsing into a fit of giggles.

"Omigod," she said, laughing as she flopped back against the booth. "The things that are coming out of me tonight! I don't know what's wrong with me."

Beatle looked at her seriously.

"I hope you don't mind me saying, but I suspect you might be a bit of a T's."

She laughed and cocked her chin.

Beatle moved towards her. His mouth close to hers.

"Hang on," Destiny said, holding a finger up to Beatle's mouth. "What's the etiquette here?"

"The etiquette?"

"You know. I met you at the tram stop. I'm just not sure what the kissing etiquette is in this type of situation."

Beatle stayed where he was, enjoying the feel of her finger on his lips. It was kind of like kissing, but not.

"No, you're right," he said. "We shouldn't."

Destiny furrowed her brow.

"You don't think so?"

"No," Beatle said. "I think you're right. I think it would be a mistake."

Destiny grinned and moved her finger away from Beatle's mouth.

"You know what they say about mistakes, though," she said, all breathy and half-lispy. "It's the only way you ever learn anything."

And she leaned forward and kissed him. Right there, in the middle of the bar. Right there, in the middle of his lips.

The smell of her, the taste of her, the feel of her, the closeness of her. Her head in his hand, her hair soft.

Only one detail jarred with the whole love and lust thing that Beatle was experiencing at that moment.

One tiny detail.

And that one tiny detail was Beatle's girlfriend.

Cilla.

*D*estiny had heard it all before:

"Finally I've met my Destiny."

"I feel like you're my Destiny."

"Does this mean we're destined to be together?"

Most of the crap lines in the world, she'd heard. So it was refreshing to meet a guy who didn't spin some cliché as soon as he heard her name.

It was one of the things she liked about Beatle. That, and the fact that he was funny and witty and had this strange little quirk about Friday the 13th, but stayed out late once he'd met her, even though he thought he was risking a major accident. And his cute face didn't hurt, either.

"So let me get this straight," Mathilde said, sitting opposite Destiny on the tram. "We've been feeling sorry for you all morning . . ."

". . . and all last night," Netta pointed out.

". . . and all last night because we didn't get you a

ticket to Blue Train, and then we find out that when you left us to go home . . ."

". . . looking so sad, walking all on your lonesome," Netta added.

". . . putting on that sad face so we all felt as bad as we possibly could . . ."

". . . which we did already anyway . . ."

". . . you then spent the night kissing some anonymous guy that you met at the tram stop," Mathilde said. "I just want to make sure I've got this right."

"That we're crystal about the whole deal," Netta added.

Destiny looked at her two buddies: Mathilde with her blonde hair pulled straight back in a ponytail so that her face was featured, and Netta, who also had blonde hair, but liked to wear hers down and kind of scruffy, as if she'd just gotten back from the beach. Netta constantly tugged at the sides of her hair to make sure it was in front of her ears and down the sides of her face, level with the edge of her eyes. Destiny suspected Netta wasn't even aware she was doing it half the time, clawing with both hands down the sides of her face to keep her hair just so.

"I didn't spend all night kissing him," Destiny said. "Just a couple of hours. It sounds much worse the way you're saying it. Like I'm some kind of skank."

"You are some kind of skank," said Mathilde.

"That's what we like about you," added Netta.

Destiny grinned.

"So what else?" said Netta, tugging her hair forward.

"What else what?"

"You know," said Mathilde. "Name, age, serial number."

Destiny leaned back against her seat and plopped her feet onto Mathilde's lap. Mathilde shoved them off and onto the seat between her and Netta.

"Well, his name's Beatle."

"Beetle?" Mathilde frowned. "What—he's got a hard shell and spindly legs?"

"Six of them?" put in Netta.

"Charming," said Destiny. "No. Actually—"

"Did you tell him he was *bugging* you when he first came up?" asked Mathilde.

"Did you tell him to *buzz* off?" asked Netta.

"When he left, did he say he had to *fly*?"

"If you really like him, just *bee* yourself."

"You'll know it's serious when he introduces you to his uncle and *ant*."

"If he ever tried to kill himself, would that be called *insecticide*?"

Destiny shifted her gaze from one to the other, like it was a tennis match.

"Are you finished yet?" she asked.

They both looked at her, but she could see their minds were still racing.

"He's called Beatle with an A," Destiny finally said. "As in The Beatles. His name's John Lennon."

"Omigod," Mathilde said.

"That's freaky," agreed Netta.

"What?" asked Destiny.

"McCartney and Lennon? You can't tell me you don't think that's freaky," said Mathilde.

"That's a definite sign," said Netta.

Destiny rolled her eyes.

Mathilde and Netta had a whole host of "signs" they looked for in any given situation. For example, "If I see a yellow car in the next five minutes, that means Josh likes me," or "If I don't step on any cracks all the way to school, I'll get a good grade on my exam."

As far as Destiny was concerned, there were no such things as signs. Fate wasn't watching out for you every step of the way, dropping little clues like bread crumbs for you to pick up and examine, maybe even pop into your mouth and chow down on. Life was what you made of it. If you met a guy and you liked him, you decided from the way he treated you whether or not he liked you. If you wanted to do well on your exams, you studied hard, simple as that. Making up your mind based on a yellow car or stepping on cracks was madness.

"Anyway, he's very cute," Destiny said, knowing full well that Mathilde and Netta were going to go into conniptions when they heard the next tidbit, "and he goes to Elwood High, and Frank is his English teacher."

"Frank?" Mathilde said. "Your Frank?"

"Your brother Frank?" Netta clarified, as if they needed it.

"The very same."

"Oh. My. God," Mathilde said.

"That's definitely a sign," said Netta.

Destiny raised her eyes to where the ads ran at the top of the tram.

"So you're going to see him again?" asked Netta. "Did he get your number?"

"Yeah."

"Of course she'll see him again," said Mathilde. And then she started clocking off the details on her fingers, making sure she had it all correct and accounted for. "His name's Lennon, hers is McCartney. Her brother teaches him English. They only met because they were at the tram stop at the same time, early on a Friday night—how often do you go home early on a Friday night?" She looked at Destiny. Destiny shook her head. "Exactly. Never. Is she going to see him again? That'd be a big fat YES."

"If my phone rings in the next two minutes," said Netta, opening her eyes wide at the very foregone-conclusion-ness of it all, "you're definitely going to see him again."

Destiny laughed.

"Don't drag me into the crappy signs and spooky whatevers that you guys get off on. If your phone rings, it means someone wants to speak to you. That's it. Not that Beatle is my *destiny* and we're going to live happily ever after."

"Why are you such a cynic?" asked Mathilde. "Why, my friend? Why?"

And just then—spookily—Netta's phone rang.

*N*ot sure if you were paying attention before, but if you were, you'll remember that Destiny's family went like this: Grace (29), Prudence (28), Patience (26), Frank (24), Faith (22), Charity (21), Hope (20), Destiny (17), and Ernest (15).

Over the years, Destiny had noticed that each kid in the family seemed to be influenced by the name they were given. They either embodied that trait, or were completely the opposite. For example, Hope was the most pessimistic in the entire family. Frank was the sneaky one, never quite telling the whole story. Grace was clumsy as all get-out, Ern was the furthest thing from earnest you could ever find anywhere. Destiny didn't believe in destiny.

But then: Prudence was prudent and Patience was patient. Charity was generous beyond reasonable. Faith had a complete and utter belief in herself, her ideas, and the importance of doing something if you think it's right.

So when Faith had a moneymaking scheme, she went right ahead and started making money off it—quite a lot of money, as it turned out. Especially for a twenty-two-year-old.

The idea she'd had was to set up a library. Except Faith didn't have a library of books. She had a library of clothes. And jewelry. And accessories.

It had all started with her friends and each of her sisters raiding her wardrobe most weekends and asking her to style them. You see, Faith was known for two things: her knack with clothes, and her hoarding of shirts, skirts, and all things fashionable. She spent most of her weekends, and most of her money, rummaging through the thrift store racks to come home with "this for fifty cents and this was quite expensive—a dollar," and would then snip, cut, and sew until the rag she'd bought was cool-beyond-cool to positively ice-cold.

As time went on, her friends' sisters, and her sisters' friends started coming over and raiding her 'robe as well. But when friends of her friends' sisters, and sisters of her sisters' friends started coming and grabbing stuff, Faith decided to charge them for the privilege. A small fee, each year, to help her buy more clothes so they'd have a wider range to choose from.

And it had gone from being this little pea-in-a-pod of an idea to a gigantic watermelon of an operation, with a client base that extended well beyond her family and friends. In fact, it had caught on so well that recently some local designers had started giving her free clothes to promote their new lines each season and she'd been mentioned on a few Web sites and blogs, and six weeks ago she'd had to open her own shop called Faith's Library, in East St Kilda off Carlisle Street, to cope with the increased demand.

Which hadn't, to be honest, suited Destiny.

Because now, instead of walking out of her bedroom door and crossing the hallway into Faith's room to pick out a little something to wear that night, she had to catch the tram all the way from home in Kew . . .

"Near Kew or far Kew?" Destiny and her buddies would ask every time. And whoever was asked would say, "far Kew," and they would all nod because this was exactly the right answer to give. (Say it out loud, and you should get it.)

. . . to Faith's little shop just off Carlisle Street in East St Kilda.

Which accounts for what Destiny, Mathilde, and Netta were doing on the tram, the morning after Destiny's night before with a boy called Beatle.

They had got off at Westbury Street and were walking down towards Faith's Library when Destiny was gripped by a random act of kindness and decided to get them all coffees.

So they walked back down to Carlisle Street and

schlepped along until they got to a shop with big baskets of coffee beans in the window and a big coffee machine on a dented-looking wooden counter and people inside drinking cups of hard-core espresso.

"Here looks good," Destiny said.

"As good as any." Mathilde shrugged.

And they went in.

And the guy behind the counter went "Hi" with a wide grin, as if he were very pleased to see them. Very pleased indeed.

And Destiny looked at him as if she were very pleased to see him. Very pleased indeed. And smiled a big smile right back.

"Destiny," he said.

"Beatle," she said.

On Saturday the fourteenth of February (also known as Valentine's Day), Destiny McCartney walked into the shop where Beatle Lennon worked—completely by coincidence.

And if you think Netta and Mathilde didn't consider that to be an absolute, no-doubt-about-it, you-guys-are-meant-to-be-together sign, you've got another think coming your way.

$\mathcal{D}$estiny had a vague feeling that it was wrong to dump her friends for a boy. But when Beatle asked if she wanted to go and do something after he'd finished his shift at the coffee shop, well, what's a girl supposed to do?

"That'd be brilliant," she said.

Of course.

Because she might not believe in Fate, but she sure did believe in going out with a cute boy if he asked her.

She dropped in at Faith's Library with Mathilde and Netta, had a breathless conversation about how cute he was . . .

"How cute is he?" she said to Mathilde.

"Very."

. . . listened to Mathilde and Netta and Faith discuss what a huge coincidence it was that of all the cafés in Melbourne, they walked into that one . . .

"Huge," said Netta.

"Enormous," said Mathilde.

. . . scoffed when they pointed out that it was Valentine's Day . . .

"The most romantic day of the year," added Mathilde somewhat irrelevantly.

"It's got to be a sign," agreed Netta.

"No doubt about it," declared Mathilde.

"You guys are meant to be together," confirmed Netta.

. . . grabbed some clothes and et ceteras to wear to Emily's party that night . . .

"This is the cutest thing," Faith said, pulling a white lace minidress off a hanger and tossing it to Destiny. "I found it in the thrift store on the corner of Carlisle Street—you know that new one—and with these," a pair of tan suede boots that stopped fetchingly at the knee, "and this," a chunky fake gold chain, "and your hair in braids, gorgeous."

. . . and got back to Beatle's café fashionably five minutes late, where he was slouched against the wall looking cute as all get-out.

*H*e took her on the perfect Valentine's Day date.

Two foot-longs (Italian herb-and-cheese roll with chicken fillet, lettuce, olives, onion and tomato, salt and pepper) from Subway and a walk down to the botanical gardens in St Kilda.

At least, she walked; he limped. She could see that he was putting all his effort into walking normally, but something with his leg wouldn't obey. His right leg would move forward in your standard step manner, but when it was his left leg's turn, it would push itself forward just a fraction quicker than it should, ready to catch the weight of his body in case his right leg couldn't handle it.

It was kind of cute.

A normal step, then a quick *stp*. Step *stp*. Step *stp*. Like an old man's leg had been attached to a young guy's body.

Very intriguing.

In a quiet corner of the botanical gardens they set up their impromtu picnic of two foot-longs and two Cokes, and Destiny sat cross-legged, looking down at his face as he lay on the grass and spoke in a low voice that seemed to rumble deep down inside his chest. He told her about how his twin sister was born two months after him (they were dyzygotes or zydygotes or something) and about being in the *Guinness World Records*, as well as hogging the front page of the paper for a day.

He had this sandy-colored hair that was a bit curly but not too much—just a bit flicky around the edges—and a mouth that dipped hugely in the middle, almost an impossible dip that made his mouth seem slightly puffy and swollen as if he'd kissed too much, and Destiny lay down beside him on the grass with her elbow propping up her head so she still had a good view of him as he spoke.

"So that's why I've got this star sign problem," he said, lolling his head over to look at her.

"What star sign problem?" she asked, flopping onto her tummy and propping her chin up on both fists.

"The problem of what star sign I should be. Should I be Sagittarius because that's when I was born, or should I be Aquarius because that's when I was supposed to be born?"

"Sagittarius definitely."

Beatle picked up a piece of her hair that was tangling down into the grass and started twisting it around his fingers.

"You think?" he said.

"Yeah. Absolutely. I'm a Leo, and Sagittarius is a perfect match for Leo."

"What about Aquarius? How does Aquarius fit with Leo?"

"Not so good, I don't think. Aquarius is better with, say, Gemini or Libra, because they're the other air signs. That's how it works. Fire goes with fire—which is why Leo and Sagittarius are a good mix—air goes with air, water with water, and earth with earth."

"And ashes to ashes, and dust to dust."

Destiny laughed. "Exactly."

Beatle shook his head.

"How come girls always know star sign shit?"

Destiny shrugged.

"I'm not really that into it. In fact, I'd go so far as to say, I think it's all bullshit. I just know a bit about it because I write an astrology column."

Beatle looked at her.

"You do not," he said.

"Do so. Every week in *Street*. Destiny Aurora-borealis-Jones."

"You're *that* Destiny? I thought it was all a made-up name."

Destiny raised an eyebrow.

"Shut up," she said. "You've never heard of me."

"I have," Beatle said, propping himself up onto his

elbow, so their faces were closer than before. "I read it quite often."

Destiny gave him her best "you're a goddamn liar" face.

"I do," he said. "And if I don't, chances are my mum will read it to me anyway. She's a freak about star signs. And numerology. And palm reading. And tarot cards. And old wives' tales. And herbal remedies. And *feng shui*—how many guys do you know who have even heard of *feng shui*, much less know how to pronounce it—and whatever you've got, she's buying."

Beatle lay back down on the grass.

"So how come you write for *Street* magazine?" he asked. "That's pretty impressive."

"Not really. My sister works there—Gracie. She's one of their writers. And the girl who used to write their column went overseas so they were stuck for someone to do it. Grace was talking about it one night at dinner, and I said how easy it would be to write, especially for someone in our family, because there's eleven of us and we've got all the star signs covered—except for Aries, but my friend Mathilde is Aries, so that's covered, too, bossy bitch that she is—and I said that I could do an astrology column in reverse sort of thing, taking what was happening to the Capricorn in our family, for example—which is my mum—and using what had happened in her week as the

basis of my column for all Capricorns. Because techni-
cally, if horoscopes are true, which I very much doubt
they are, one Capricorn's week should be about the same
as all Capricorns' weeks. You know what I mean?"

She pulled out a strand of grass and started peeling it
with her fingernail.

"Anyway, Grace thought it was a great idea—kind of
weird, which she liked, so she asked me to write a column,
as a test, for one week. So I looked up a couple of astrology Web sites to get the jargon right and then just wrote
about what was happening to each person in our family. And Grace took it in and the editor really liked it, so
I've been doing it ever since. And it's kind of fun, because
it's like our family's own personal newsletter, published
each week in *Street*. So if, say, Frank hasn't been home
all week, he can still catch up on what's been happening
with, say, Prue, by reading about Scorpios."

Her sample column—the one that got her the gig—
had gone along these lines:

LIBRA (Frank)

**With Venus in retrograde, I think you've got your head up
Uranus. Get back with Josie—she's a great girl.**

SCORPIO (Prue)

**Don't know what planet you were on when you
decided to get that last haircut of yours. The good news is:
it'll grow.**

SAGITTARIUS (Gracie)

It's written in your stars that you will help your sister get a job with your magazine. Repeat after me: get her a job, get her a job.

And so on and so forth through the entire zodiac, finishing with:

LEO (Destiny)

As one of the zodiac's fire signs, you have a burning ambition to write horoscopes for *Street* magazine. You have the spark they need.

Surprisingly, they bought it.

Even more surprising, her column had proven to be reasonably popular. Not hugely, but reasonably. No one in the general reading public seemed to put much store in her words of wisdom, but they all seemed to quite like the reality-TV-soap-opera-ish aspect of it all. In fact, a recent column had resulted in Patience receiving a torrent of letters from prospective suitors. Well, not a torrent exactly. Three. But still, Destiny felt that was an amazingly positive response to her work.

Patience hadn't been so happy.

"I can't believe you," Patience had said across the dinner table. "Seriously. Don't use me in your columns anymore. I forbid it."

"What? You can't forbid it, because I never got your permission in the first place. Besides, I think it's sweet that these guys are writing, offering to take you out."

"It's embarrassing. I don't want everyone knowing my private life. I'm serious. Don't use my name any more."

So Destiny had written a column for Pisces the next week that read:

PISCES (Patience)

My apology is rising in the ascendant. I'm sorry. Please, can I keep using your name? The column won't be the same without you.

Patience got three more letters from the same three guys and an even steelier resolve for her name not to be used.

So now Pisces was written for "Deborah," but it was still Patience just the same.

Destiny was coming up on her first anniversary as Destiny Auroraborealis-Jones and felt that she had become a lot more knowledgeable about the whole astrology business. She had learned the difference between sun signs and ascendant signs and that the Moon and Mercury and Venus and Mars and Jupiter and Saturn and Uranus and Neptune and Pluto all have an impact on a person's birth chart. She knew that Virgos were tidy and Leos were arrogant and Cancerians were sensitive. Well, you'd be sensitive, too, if your star sign was the name of a deadly disease. She knew that the time and place of birth impacted on your chart, as well as the day and year you were born.

She knew all this. She just didn't believe any of it.

Beatle butted into her thoughts. "So why Aurora-borealis-Jones?"

Destiny bit her lip.

"Dunno. Well, the Destiny part's obvious, and then Auroraborealis—we were trying to think of something as New Age-y as we possibly could, and the aurora borealis are the Northern Lights—you know?"

Beatle watched her mouth as she spoke, making her feel self-conscious and her lips twitchy.

"They happen in, like, Scandinavia and Iceland and around there," she said. "These amazing light shows that have something to do with magnetic energy, I think."

"Yeah. Like in that Philip Pullman book."

"Exactly. And then Jones, well," she continued in a rush, "that was just because the whole Destiny Auroraborealis sounded so out-there, we thought Jones brought it all back down to earth."

Beatle put his hand on the back of her head and brought her face over to him, all the better to kiss her. A long, slow kiss that seemed to have lots of words in it, and lots of getting-to-know-you in it, and by the time he let her have her lips back, she could hardly breathe.

"You ever heard of Dave Gorman?" Beatle asked, brushing her neck with barely-there kisses.

"Dave Gorman?" she asked, all breathless.

"He's this English guy," Beatle said into her collarbone. "He's"—kiss—"this"—kiss—"English"—kiss—"guy"—kiss.

"Ah," she said, not really paying attention to the words.

"He did an astrology experiment. Called it Dave Gorman's Important Astrology Experiment."

"Catchy title," she said, laughing. "How do you think he came up with it?"

Beatle grinned.

"He followed his daily horoscopes religiously for forty days and did exactly what they told him to do. If they said he was going to back a winner that day, he'd go to the races and put some money down."

Destiny watched him talk.

"If they said he was going on a long trip, he'd hop on a plane and go to New York. You get the picture. But to balance the project and make it more scientific-like, he used his identical twin brother as a control experiment. His brother completely ignored his horoscopes and made decisions based on what he felt like doing. Each week a panel assessed the two brothers to see who was happier, healthier, and wealthier."

"Did it work?" Destiny asked, only keeping the conversation going because it was the polite thing to do, when really all she wanted was for him to kiss her more.

"Well, Dave Gorman's life was infinitely more successful, obviously. He had a TV show and everything. But even without the TV show, he won. The panel judged him the winner. He maintained that he only won by a smidge, but still, he won."

"How do you know all this?" she asked.

"Mental mother," he said, shaking his head.

And then he brought his lips back to hers and started kissing her again.

*H*ere is a list of things that were doing Beatle's head in:

#1: Meeting a girl called Destiny on Friday the 13th.

#2: Meeting a girl called Destiny whose last name was McCartney—the yin to his Lennon yang.

#3: Meeting a girl called Destiny on the only night of the weekend that his girlfriend, Cilla, could get in to use the darkroom at school.

#4: The fact that Destiny wouldn't have even been at the stop at the same time as him if she hadn't been given a detention earlier in the week.

#5: The fact that she had left her glasses in her friend's bag, which meant she had to wear her sunglasses to read her book, which meant he'd had to make a comment, which meant they'd had to have a conversation, which meant they'd had to get a drink, which meant they'd had to chat more, which meant he'd had to kiss her. Had to. Couldn't help himself.

#6: The fact that she then came into the café for the first time ever the next day, Saturday the fourteenth of February, which also happens to be known as Valentine's Day. The day of lovers. . . .

#7: If she'd come in seven minutes later, he'd have finished his shift and would have left for the day. He wasn't even supposed to be working—he and Cilla were supposed to have gone to the movies—but his boss had asked him that morning because one of the other guys had called in sick.

#8: He had a girlfriend.

#9: HE HAD A GIRLFRIEND. If he had a girlfriend, and if he was supposedly in love with that girlfriend, what was he doing kissing another girl?

#10: He had a girlfriend who was really sweet.

#11: An important one—his girlfriend hadn't treated him like a freak after he had his stroke.

*B*eatle held Cilla's hand as they walked through Camberwell Market that Sunday morning and hoped to hell all the thoughts that were sloshing around inside his head weren't flashing up like big neon signs across his face.

Cilla looked at him, and he looked away. Just in case she saw something. A clue of some sort. Anything that would make her think "unfaithful" and "Beatle" in the same sentence.

This morning, before they'd come to Camberwell Market, Beatle had settled himself down at the kitchen table and flicked casually to the astrology section. A casual opening-up-the-newspaper thing. Not a specifically-searching-out-the-horoscopes-because-he-didn't-know-what-to-do-about-cheating-on-his-girlfriend type thing. Aquarius had read: "Today's lunar-solar polarities could produce a conflict between personal and worldly drives, resulting in a lack of clarity, fuzzy focus, or shifting priorities. Be really clear about what's important to you."

And that was the thing he had to remember: what was really important to him was Cilla.

Cilla was smart. The very first thing he'd ever noticed about Cilla was how smart she was. You could tell—even by the way she said "Hi" in that offhand, deep, distracted voice of hers, and the way she glanced at you briefly from under her eyelashes—that she was a smart girl.

And she was tiny, she could just about sit in your hand, which Beatle found particularly attractive. Especially when it was coupled with her personality, which was so big. Admittedly, she could be a bitch when she wanted to be, but she never said anything unless it was well deserved. There was no chit-chatty small talk for Cilla. Everything was BIG. Real. Thoughtful.

And she was down to earth. She never glammed herself up. Sometimes she might wear crazy clothes, but never glam. Sometimes she'd get to school and her hair would look a bit bumpy, like she hadn't even brushed it. But even her bumpy hair, Beatle liked.

And she was a Libran, which meant they were perfectly well suited. Two air signs: Libra and Aquarius. A match made in astrology heaven.

Unless he was a Sagittarius, of course; in which case, things weren't quite so clear-cut.

Sagittarius had read: "The time has come for decisions to be made. For too long you've coasted along without actively arranging your world. Saturn is in line with Uranus," Beatle would defy anyone not to smirk to themselves when they read that word, "so now is the time to choose the path that is right for you."

And that path would be . . . ?

Beatle had sat at the kitchen table, looking at the pictures beside each sign. The fish. The ram. The lion. The twins. He liked the whole symbolism of the zodiac. For example, you didn't have to be a brainiac to figure that Leo with Pisces was always going to be doomed. Because the thing is, Leo is a lion—in other words, a big cat—and Pisces is a fish, and guess what? Cats eat fish. For dinner. Or breakfast. Or lunch. Or whatever meal happens to be going at the time. And take Aries, for another example. The ram. Well, you got a pretty clear picture of personality right from the start.

He looked at Sagittarius: the archer. Half man, half horse. Not the kind of imagery that spoke of stability and sensibleness. In fact, with his bow and arrow and half-half body, he was always going to be a screwup and a bit dangerous, too. Beatle would be willing to bet the archer regularly snuck around in the heavens, kissing other girls when his girlfriend wasn't around.

Beatle didn't want to be a sneaking-around-kissing-other-girls type guy.

Beatle intertwined his fingers with Cilla's and chucked his chin in the direction of the donut van.

"Hungry?" he asked.

Not that he particularly wanted a donut himself, but he needed to concoct some reason for avoiding Cilla's gaze, and if donuts were the first thing that came to mind, then donuts it was.

Cilla frowned at him.

"You're not supposed to have that kind of stuff," she said.

"It'll be fine."

He tucked Cilla in under his arm and headed over to stand in the line.

And actually, the donuts smelled good once he got closer. Damn good. Hot jam and sugar and cinnamon and dough all blobbed together in a big, fat hit of junk. Exactly what he needed.

Exactly what he wasn't supposed to have.

Here is another list, that used to do Beatle's head in, but doesn't anymore because he's used to it:

#1: Eat healthy and exercise regularly but not to extreme.

#2: Avoid fats, especially the ones in meat and butter. And probably the ones in donuts.

(Definitely the ones in donuts.)

#3: Monitor your blood pressure.

#4: Check your cholesterol.

#5: Test your blood sugar. Chronic high blood sugar is bad for arteries. Donuts probably aren't that hot for them, either.

#6: Don't smoke.

#7: An important one—don't binge on drugs or alcohol. This was the one he felt worst about. Because smoking weed was what he'd been doing the night he'd had his stroke. And the worst thing about *that* was his mom.

"Your brain isn't properly formed until you're twenty-three, did you know that?" she'd said only a couple of weeks before he'd had his stroke as they sat at the table having breakfast. Beatle had looked over at her and done his "Ah, isn't that interesting" face while Winsome had raised her eyes and done her "Who gives a shit" face.

His mom had tapped the newspaper, pointing to the article she was reading. Beatle was grateful it wasn't the horoscopes for once. For that small mercy, he was grateful.

"And because of that—it says here—it's very dangerous for children to binge drink or take drugs. Children, as in teenagers," she'd added, in case they weren't clear on who she was talking about.

"Right," Beatle had said.

"Or children, obviously," she conceded.

"God. You think we're idiots," Winsome had said, her lip curling as she tucked her Cheerios in.

"No. I don't think you're idiots. I think you're teenagers. And teenagers take risks—that's their job. But drinking can cause brain damage," their mom said, reading directly from the newspaper, "and smoking dope,"—she always called it "dope," which seemed so kind of wrong and old-fashioned and weird coming out of her mouth—"can cause schizophrenia." She tapped the words as she read them. "So," she said, looking up, "it's very important not to binge drink or do drugs."

"Do drugs." That had sounded weird, too. Beatle remembered it had been impossible to take her seriously.

She always did things ass-backwards, his mom. Lecturing about drugs when they were having breakfast. Talking about homework when they were on vacation. Asking what they were doing about getting a job when it was nighttime and there was nothing they could do about it. "Promise me," she'd said, "you won't drink too much or take drugs."

Winsome had clicked her tongue at their mom and dismissed her with an "I'm not even going to enter into this discussion" look.

Beatle had held up his pinky finger and said, "Pinky-swear, I won't binge drink or do drugs." A flippant pledge, a spontaneous gesture. It had seemed harmless enough at the time. It hadn't meant anything. But as it turned out, he'd jinxed himself badly. Here's the lesson:

God pays back those who pinky-swear and go back on their word.

A couple of weeks later he'd been over at Bollo's house with Toby and Magnus and a couple of others having a smoke, when he'd gotten this gigantic headache banging against the inside of his skull and his arm had gone numb, like he'd lain on it and it had gone to sleep. It didn't hurt or anything, just felt numb. And then the feeling had travelled all the way down his body, all the way down the right side. A strange, tranquil, numb feeling down one half of his body.

"I'm whacked," he'd said, his voice slurring. He tried to move his fingers. But only the fingers on his left hand wiggled. His right-hand fingers lay there like they were full of sand. He stared at them and started giggling, even though his head hurt like hell. "This is weird," he'd said, the words not quite coming out right. Toby had looked over at him and grinned, and Bollo had said, "Good stuff, yeah?" as if they'd really gotten their money's worth, then started rolling another one.

Beatle got his money's worth, all right. He went to stand up but fell onto the floor instead. Bollo cracked up, Toby looked at him with glazed eyes and a grin. Only Magnus leaned forward and asked, "Are you okay, man?"

He had double vision, the right side of his body felt like it was a sack of skin filled with jelly-for-bones, and he couldn't talk. He started suspecting this was more than your average trip.

"Call my mum," he said, his tongue feeling like it was too thick for his mouth. And then he said, "No, don't. I'll be alright."

But Magnus didn't seem to be hearing him. Or understanding him, at least. He had knelt down beside Beatle and tried to get him to stand, but Beatle was useless. "Fuck," he remembered Magnus saying. "Fuck," a tinge entering his voice that Beatle had never heard before. "Something's wrong with Beatle."

"He's stoned," Bollo said. "He never smokes. He's not used to it."

"No," Magnus said. "This is bad. Get him some coffee."

And all the while Beatle had lain there, face planted into the carpet, thinking how strange it was that he couldn't move and wondering whether this was schizophrenia and how he was going to explain to his mom that he'd smoked weed when he'd pinky-sworn he wouldn't.

It was when he couldn't drink the coffee that they'd all started taking it seriously.

Magnus had called Winsome, who was over at Cilla's place.

Beatle could remember being vaguely interested in a

detached way that he didn't even feel embarrassed when the girls walked in and saw him sprawled on the ground.

"Shit," Winsome had said and called their mother.

Who had called an ambulance.

Which had taken him to the hospital.

Winsome had gone in the ambulance with him, and their mom had met them at the hospital. And burst into tears as soon as she looked at him.

And again he'd thought—with detachment—how strange it was that he didn't seem to be feeling any of the emotions he'd have expected to feel.

He was in the hospital for a couple of weeks. The doctors told him that his friends should have called an ambulance right away. That he'd had a stroke and the quicker you treat these things, the better. And still Beatle hadn't felt anything. Not anger, or shame, or humiliation, or frustration, or anything. Only blankness.

As if his soul had left his body.

After a couple of weeks, he was sent to rehab and put on antidepressants. He told them he wasn't depressed—he just wished he wasn't alive, didn't see any point to anything. He couldn't play sports. Jesus, he couldn't move his arm and leg, he still had double vision, he choked every time he drank, and he couldn't talk properly. If anything, it was perfectly reasonable and normal for him to wish he wasn't alive. It wasn't depression: it was reality.

But they'd put him on antidepressants, and he'd started having physical therapy, and speech therapy and occupational therapy, and his leg had started to move, but his foot still felt numb. Then he'd wiggled his toes one day, which was a good sign, and he'd been able to bend his arm a bit, which everyone said was great, but he didn't *really* think it was great because it was useless compared to how it had been before his stroke. Then his vision had started to get better—still a bit blurry, but it didn't make him feel nauseous to look at things—and he'd learned how to swallow drinks and started going to the bathroom on his own and he'd be wheeled each morning into the physical therapy center and he started walking; weird, plonky steps because his foot still felt numb and he was scared of falling.

And he started feeling better. He told his mom he'd be happy to see some of his friends. Not everyone, just his good buddies.

And when Toby and Magnus first came they brought chocolates, which seemed so lame and stupid, as if it were a first date, and he'd said, "What? No flowers?" but they hadn't understood what he was saying, because his speech was still slurry, and "flowers" came out like "fhluuus." Then when he'd repeated it, they still hadn't gotten it, and he repeated it again, but it didn't sound funny anymore, because no joke sounds funny when it's told three times, and they still didn't understand what he was saying anyway.

Beatle had thought—after that first time—he wouldn't see them again, but they had surprised him. Every day at about quarter past four they'd walk into his room and throw their schoolbags on the floor, toss their skateboards on top, and then tell him about what had gone on at school that day and what some freak on the tram had done when they were on their way over to the hospital, and he'd show them that he could walk a bit better today, or that his arm was starting to move and that his fingers were wiggling whenever his brain gave the command, or tell them what their favorite nurse, the one whose uniform hugged her just so, had said that day about his vital signs.

And Toby would cup his hands palms-up at groin height and say, "Has she checked out all your vital signs?" and the three of them would crack up.

Beatle knew he was well down the road to recovery when his friends gave him shit about some word his tongue was having trouble getting around or mimicked the way he walked or picked up something with a cramped, clawed hand.

And then Cilla started coming in with Winsome.

And a couple of times she came in on her own.

And then, one day when he was pissed off at rehab

and pissed off at his body and his mouth wasn't working properly and his words were coming out all flunky, she'd sat on the bed beside him and leaned her mouth down to kiss his.

Just at the point when he was starting to feel well enough to feel pissed off, she'd kissed him and made him feel better.

Just at the point when he'd resigned himself to the fact that no girl was ever going to want to be with a freak like him, she'd made him feel normal.

So at what point had he decided it was okay to betray Cilla by kissing another girl?

He knew Cilla would never do it to him. (Although the thought of Cilla kissing another girl wasn't something he'd say no to.)

Cilla was sweet and kind and smart, and she worried a lot about all kinds of things; she worried about how she was doing in her senior year, and whether she'd get into college, and if she didn't, what would she do, and could she afford to go to college anyway when it was going to cost her about a million bucks a year, and should she get her tongue pierced and what if it got infected. The only thing she didn't worry about was whether she could trust Beatle.

She trusted him to tell her the truth when she had her hair dyed black and cut into a choppy bob.

He said he liked it, even though he didn't really.

She trusted him to tell her the truth about whether he liked her nose pierced or not.

He said he liked it, and he did really.

She trusted him when he said he'd gone home early on Friday night while she was working late in the darkroom.

She trusted him when he said he'd been working all day yesterday at the café.

She trusted him when he was late to pick her up last night for Matt's party and said it was because he'd gotten home late from work.

She trusted him.

And he was completely untrustworthy.

*T*wins sit on chairs beside each other. Their names appear on the bottom of the screen: "Mark" and "Eric." Two good-looking guys who have the distinction of being indistinguishable from each other.

One of them—"Mark"—is speaking.

"I was born forty-five seconds before him," he says. "I think it's important to mention that before we go any further."

"He always says that," Eric says. "It's the first thing he tells people. As if anyone cares."

"Oh, they care all right. People care," Mark says, grinning. "They care very much indeed."

"Anyway." Eric shakes his head.

"Anyway," Mark agrees, "we were flat broke, living in a house in Carlton, studying full time. Working at a pub in the city. But then Eric heard about a job at this big law firm. They wanted someone to work full time on research."

"But neither of us," Eric butts in, "could work full time—we had classes to go to. So we came up with the inspired idea of job-sharing."

"Except we didn't tell them that," says Mark, a laugh bubbling up in his throat.

"It worked perfectly," says Eric. "If Mark had a class in the morning, I'd work, then we'd meet up at lunchtime, he'd change into the clothes I'd been wearing that morning, then he'd go into work and finish off the day."

Mark rubs his chin thoughtfully, then picks up the thread of the story where Eric has left it.

"Once we got over the initial weirdness," Mark goes on. "Say, for example, when someone would talk about 'you know, that thing we were talking about yesterday,' and I wouldn't have a clue what they were talking about. . . ."

"I acted a bit vague when they said something like that," says Eric.

"He does a scarily convincing vague—almost too convincing," says Mark. "So apart from that, things were going along until . . ."

And here Eric grins.

". . . Sonya came along."

"Which didn't sit all that well with my girlfriend," continues Mark. "Because this chick, Sonya, would flirt with me, thinking I was Eric."

Eric leans forward, resting his elbow on his knee.

"So this one night," Eric says, taking up the thread, "Sonya saw what she thought was me heading into a pub after work and followed me in."

"Except it wasn't him," chimes in Mark, "was it? It was me. Catching up with my girlfriend, Melissa."

"Try explaining that to the chick you're having a fling with: that you've actually got a twin brother, who you forgot to mention."

"We both lost our jobs," says Mark, "seeing as Sonya's dad was one of the senior partners, and it was all a bit dodgy what we were doing. Sonya and Eric didn't last either. Surprisingly. Something about how she couldn't trust him."

And the two twins grin at each other like naughty little boys.

The interviewer mumbles something.

"Now that's an interesting question, isn't it?" Eric says, raising an eyebrow. "Which only Mark can answer. Did he sleep with Sonya when she thought he was me? Who knows? He says he didn't, and Sonya says she doesn't think he did, and Melissa says he promised her he didn't, but . . ." and he leaves the sentence hanging in the air between them.

"I didn't," Mark says, opening his palms wide in

the universal body language of I-don't-have-anything-to-hide. "I've already said I didn't sleep with her."

But then there's the tiniest smirk. You'd hardly notice it. Almost a twitch, it's so quick. But it's there. A definite grin. Right in the middle of his face.

The Yarra River meanders through Kew towards the bay with the same indolent swagger that can be found on most of the private school boys and girls that live in the area. Kew's that kind of place—the kind of place where even the waterways have attitude and a sense of privilege. With its wide streets and its more-tennis-courts-more-swimming-pools-and-way-less-poor-people-per-capita demographic. When you live in Kew, you expect everyone to have a house with at least two stories, four bedrooms, a study, a formal dining room, a formal living room, and an extremely generous allowance doled out to the 2.4 children that live there.

The preferred dog in Kew is the golden retriever.

Which accounts for the two golden retrievers at the end of Mathilde's and Destiny's leashes as they walked down Destiny's street. Past the O'Hallorans' (2 stories, 3 children, 1 swimming pool), the Nagles' (2 stories, 2 children, 1 swimming pool, and 1 tennis court), the Fetherston-haughs' (2 stories, 2 children, 1 swimming pool), and the Hannigans' (2 stories, no children, lazy rolling lawns).

And in front of Mrs. Sheffield's place (2 stories, 2 grown children, 6 grandkids, 1 massive old tree in the front yard), sitting on the sidewalk like a surreal drawing room scene under the old oak tree, was an ornately carved chair with a cross-stitch tapestry seat.

Destiny and Mathilde both stopped to look at it.

"We'll have to go for a walk tomorrow night. Get Netta to come. See what else people are throwing out," Destiny said.

Rummaging through garbage was a pretty regular thing for the three of them. Netta liked searching for bits that she could put on necklaces and earrings. Mathilde was always on the hunt for old suitcases and lamps. And Destiny was constantly on the lookout for interesting trash that she could make sculptures out of for art class. She'd made this particularly good one last year: a janitor-type man, using the knobs off an old washing machine for eyes, the keys of a computer keyboard wrapped around his head for hair (she thought that was particularly clever, representing the brain as well as hair), and an old mower blade for his mustache.

She got an A+ for her end-of-year grade. Not to brag or anything.

Destiny had a good look at the chair, sitting on its own without any accompanying side table or couch or footstool. Walked around it, kicked at the curlicued legs, waggled the back (it was loose—obviously the reason it was being thrown out), folded her arms in front of her chest, and thought for a moment.

"Actually," she said, squatting down and checking the underside of the chair, "this could be perfect for my art project."

"What? Another sculpture?"

"No. Not the whole chair. Although maybe…" Destiny considered it for a moment. "No, I've been wanting to do a series of paintings this year. But I could use the rest of it to make a sculpture—the legs for legs, the back for the body, the arms for arms, maybe. Anyway, you know how the theme I've chosen is Home?"

"Yeah."

"And I wasn't quite sure—thought it was a bit lame or whatever. But looking at this, I think it might be quite good. I mean, tapestries generally represent Home pretty much, don't they? And this one, with the picture of the house, is kind of perfect. So if I put this on a canvas—took it off the seat, so it's flat, and then stapled it—or maybe even stitched it, that could look quite good, with kind of fluorescent thread—but pull out some threads and make it look all kind of damaged and a bit angry, maybe even paint over it with graffiti or something, that could be pretty cool, I think, and represent Home not necessarily being a place of sanctuary anymore, but more a place of conflict and . . . yeah, so whaddya think?"

Mathilde frowned at her, and Destiny could tell she was deciding whether to make a joke, a smart-ass comment, or take her seriously for once.

"Can you repeat that? Just from 'I've got a good idea.'"

Destiny ignored her.

"I mean, I can still do idealistic representations of Home as well, like surburbia, but this one, and maybe one other, can represent Home for kids who end up living on the streets. 'Cause surely their idea of Home would be very fractured and angry and yeah, I think it could be quite good."

Mathilde seemed to be taking her seriously for a moment.

"Should I ask Mrs. Sheffield if I can have it?" Destiny said.

Mathilde scrunched up her face. "She's such an old bat. She'll say no, just because you want it."

Destiny nodded. Never a truer word had been spoken.

"And it's broken," Mathilde pointed out. "She obviously doesn't want it."

"Yeah."

"If you ask and she says no—you can't take it. If you don't ask, she can't say no—which means you can have it."

"That's true."

"You're doing her a favor."

"Well, I would be. You're right."

The very fact that someone else wanted it would be enough to make Mrs. Sheffield keep it from them. She'd look down her hawkish, bent nose at Destiny and say, "No, I don't think so, dear," even though there wasn't anything dear to her about Destiny at all. She'd say she was worried that Destiny would hurt herself on it, or that there were termites in the wood and that's why she was throwing it out, or that it was so ruined she couldn't possibly give it to her. No matter how much Destiny wanted it, no matter that it was for her art project, Mrs. Sheffield would brick-wall her.

So Destiny picked up the chair without asking and carried it into her house and up to her bedroom, while Mathilde, Pepsi, and Fido served as lookouts.

Yes, Fido. Only Mathilde's family could be so cruel as to name their family dog Fido. Pepsi—you'd agree—is a much more sensible name for the family pet.

Up in the safety of Destiny's bedroom, Mathilde sat on the floor as Destiny pulled the tapestry off the cushion and flattened it out on her bed.

"It's old, that's for sure," said Mathilde.

"Look at the stitches. Even the back of it," Destiny said, turning it over, "is perfect. I wonder who did it?"

"Some old duck."

"Mrs. Sheffield, do you think?"

"Can't imagine her having the patience," said

Mathilde. "She'd have poked someone's eye out with the needle before she was finished."

Destiny grinned.

It was a lovely scene, made up of the tiniest stitches you ever saw in your life. Each stitch no bigger than an eyelash and no longer than a pinhead. There was a house in the middle of the picture, a double-story joint with a Juliet balcony and a garden that went beyond the house to the fields on the left, where cows were munching on grass and butterflies were lighting on flowers. Across the top were embroidered the words "Home is where the heart is" in calligraphy stitching, as if it had been written with a pen.

"It almost seems a shame to cut it," Destiny said, wondering whether she should change the concept. Maybe this was one of the representations of the idealistic Home, not the antithesis of it.

"Yeah, but if you don't cut it, it doesn't mean anything. It's just your standard tapestry. Once you cut it, it gets an edge. Becomes a hard-core piece of art. You've gotta cut it," said Mathilde.

It was true. Without some cuts through it, it was only a tapestry. Beautiful, and fantastically well made, but nonetheless, a boring old tapestry.

Destiny picked up the scissors from her desk.

"Makes it more cutting edge, pardon the pun," she said, snipping around the word "home."

"Voilà," Destiny said, holding the square of fabric up as if in triumph, but feeling a squeeze of guilt that she'd now destroyed something that someone a long time ago had spent time and care over.

Destiny used the point of the scissors to pull out a couple of threads, leaving them hanging limply from the scene. She held the scissors in her fist and hacked carefully into the tapestry, giving it a raw, angry look.

And then her mom called up the stairs.

"Destiny?"

"Yeah?" she called back.

"When you were walking Pepsi, did you notice a chair outside Mrs. Sheffield's?"

Destiny looked at Mathilde, her eyes and mouth wide.

"No," called out Destiny, after a moment.

"You didn't see anyone, did you?" her mom yelled. "Actually, can you come down?" she said.

Destiny stood up and waited for Mathilde to get up, too. Mathilde sat on the floor, shaking her head, refusing to get up.

"Get up."

"No way."

"Get up. I'm not going down there by myself," hissed Destiny.

"I'm not coming. She'll guess. One look at my guilty face, and she'll know we took it."

"You're coming," said Destiny, hauling Mathilde to her feet.

They walked down to where Destiny's mom stood with her elbows on the banister.

"Poor old thing," Destiny's mom said quietly as they walked towards the kitchen. "Her son had come to take it to get repaired, but he couldn't fit it in the backseat because it was too big, so he left it in the yard while he went to borrow his brother's car—"

They were in the kitchen by this point, and there was Mrs. Sheffield, a ginormous tumbler of wine clutched in her spindly claws, gigantic diamonds showing-off on her fingers.

"I was sitting on it," Mrs. Sheffield interrupted, "waiting for him to come back, but then I heard my telephone ringing inside . . ."

Everyone in the neighborhood could hear when Mrs. Sheffield's phone rang. Her sons had rigged up some kind of outdoor speaker system so no matter where she was in the house or garden, she could hear if someone was calling her.

". . . and I went to answer it, thinking it might be him. It wasn't. It was one of those . . . those . . . you know, trying to sell time-shares and whatnot?"

She looked impatiently at Destiny.

"Um . . . telemarketers?" Destiny suggested.

"Exactly." She scowled at Destiny, as if she herself had

been responsible for the call. "And when I came back, the chair was gone."

"Oh," said Destiny.

Mathilde clicked her tongue in sympathy.

"It's very valuable," Mrs. Sheffield continued, scowling now at Mathilde as if she were the one who'd stolen it. Which she was, but Mrs. Sheffield didn't know that. "Mrs. Simpson, Wallis Simpson—she married King Edward—made it for my mother."

"Omigod," said Destiny under her breath.

"Anyway," Mrs. Sheffield went on, rapping at the table with her wizened fingers, "did you see anyone? Your mother said you came home about the time it would have happened."

Destiny looked at Mathilde and chewed on her lip.

"Actually," Mathilde said, glancing pointedly at Destiny, "there was a big four-wheel-drive that took off just as we turned into the street."

Destiny glanced at Mathilde, then across at Mrs. Sheffield.

"Kind of a blue color, I think," Mathilde added.

Mrs. Sheffield drew her eyebrows together.

"Dark blue," Destiny noted, to sound convincing.

"Definitely," said Mathilde. "Kind of a midnight blue with metallic paint."

Mrs. Sheffield looked as if she couldn't believe her

ears, then abruptly slapped the top of the table, nearly giving Destiny a heart attack.

"That'd be Susan. Antony's ex-wife," she said with a down-turned mouth for the word *Susan*. "She must have driven past, seen it, and taken it. I'll have to tell Antony. He'll have to get it back from her."

"Oh, well, it might not have been her," Destiny said, feeling the whole thing tail-spinning like a doomed plane towards the earth, a pilot shouting "mayday, mayday" as it crashed and burned on the kitchen table. "It could have been anyone. In fact, I'm not even sure the car stopped. We didn't really see it stop, not parked by the side of the road anyway, did we, Mathilde? And no one got out, I'm sure."

Mathilde thought for a moment.

"Well . . . yeah. No, it was definitely stopped. For sure. And I'm pretty sure I saw the driver's side door shutting as we turned the corner."

"It was her all right," said Mrs. Sheffield, her eyes picturing her evil ex-daughter-in-law snatching the chair as she spoke. "She's an opportunistic sneak. Wait until I tell Antony."

"But you don't know it was her for sure," said Destiny.

"No. I know it was her. I've never trusted her. And now I've got proof. There's no question."

And Mrs. Sheffield downed her wine in a strangely satisfied manner.

*T*here's a saying: what's bred in the bone.

It means that there are certain character traits that are hardwired into your system, that run through your skeleton, that are stored in your DNA, and no matter how hard you try to deny them, they're bred into your bone and will come out one way or another.

Which was exactly what Beatle was afraid of.

When Beatle's mom had been pregnant with him and Winsome, his dad had been having a full-on affair with one of the models he'd been working with. And his mom hadn't had a clue. Had just been busily incubating his two children. It was only when Michelle—the affairee—had sent a letter to Beatle's mom that she'd been clued in to what was going on. And it had gone down in their family lore.

"I remember when your father," their mom would start, and Beatle and Winsome would shrink inside so that only the tiniest part of them would hear the rest of it. Because they knew what was coming. "I remember when your father" never finished on a positive note. It never ended with their dad being a great guy, and the family having a rollicking good time somewhere.

"I remember when your father" would meander through various tales before landing at exactly the same spot. Landing at "and when I read that letter I just couldn't believe it. I was driving to his studio when I had the accident. And that's why you were born so early," she'd say, looking fondly at Beatle. "And it was just luck that the doctors managed to keep you inside for another six weeks," she'd say, smiling at Winsome, "but of course, while I was in the hospital for those six weeks, your father"—"your father" dumped unceremoniously on the floor—"moved out. Moved in with that woman."

Beatle's mom wasn't what you'd call a bounce-back-and-move-on type person. She was the type who stayed fixed to one emotional spot, long after that spot had shifted. People would come and go around her, but she remained fixed to where she was. And where she was fixed was to Beatle's dad, Michael.

Even though he had moved out to a different place by the time Beatle's mom had come home with the twins, Michael was still her compass, her focal point. The weight she'd put on, the whole astrology thing, everything stemmed from Michael.

She'd been blindsided and was determined never

to be taken by surprise again. Hence, the astrology. She checked her chart constantly, and every move she made was dictated by the stars.

As for her weight . . .

"The problem," she maintained, when she got onto the frequent topic of "your father," "was he's a very visual person—being a photographer, he would be. He fell for the look of me, not the actual person."

So she'd rectified that by stacking on the pounds. No one was ever going to fall for her looks again. She still had a very pretty face, Beatle thought, but certainly the physical boundaries established by her stomach and her breasts staked the personality patch fairly convincingly.

Although interestingly—despite her claims of not wanting to be judged on how she looked—she still kept quite a few shots from her modelling days framed and hung on the walls around their apartment.

So the whole question of what was "bred in the bone" was a real quandary for Beatle. And he didn't like how close he was cutting it at this particular moment in his life.

The question was, exactly what part of your parents is bred in you, and what isn't? Do you get a bit of your dad's personality, or the whole thing? Do you get his creativity or your mom's? Do you get your mom's obsessive behavior or your dad's charm?

What exactly were you made up of? Slugs and snails and puppy-dog tails would be far preferable to what Beatle feared was starting to seep out through his pores.

Beatle decided there was only one thing to do. He needed to show the world, his girlfriend—and himself—what a great guy he was.

So on Sunday he bought Cilla a sterling silver ring for her nose.

On Monday he bought her a can of Coke.

On Tuesday it was a Happy Meal.

And today, Wednesday, he bought her your traditional dozen long-stemmed red roses: admired and bequeathed by lovers the world over.

And that's when the trouble started.

They'd been walking home from school down Ormond Road—Cilla, Beatle, Toby, Magnus, Winsome, and Angela—and when they got up to the florist on the corner of Normandy Road, Beatle, on an impulse, bought Cilla a bunch of long-stemmed red roses (see line starting "And today, Wednesday").

Cilla stared at him.

"What's going on?" she asked, holding the flowers away from her as if they'd been dusted with anthrax.

"What do you mean?"

"All this week, you've been buying me things. And now, I mean, roses, like seriously, what's going on?"

Beatle stood in Ormond Road, arms slack by his sides, a bunch of thorny red roses between him and his girlfriend.

"Well, shit," he said, a sharp tang to his voice. "If a guy can't buy his girlfriend flowers without her getting all suspicious and weird, then fuck, what hope is there? I was trying to do the right thing, and I'm sorry if being a good guy makes you feel all . . . I don't know. But one thing I know for sure: that's the last bunch you get. I thought girls were supposed to say 'Thanks' when their boyfriends buy them flowers, not 'What the fuck are these?'"

"Beatle," Winsome said, putting her nose in where it most certainly wasn't wanted, "presents are a definite guilty sign. Next thing you'll be buying her lingerie, which is a dead giveaway."

"Is that true?" Toby asked, frowning at Winsome.

"That's what the magazines say," Winsome answered, shrugging. "A guilty conscience is an open wallet."

Thanks, Winsome. You are really helping the cause, thought Beatle.

"As opposed to a clean conscience, which is a soft pillow," Winsome continued.

Yeah. Right. Whatever.

Cilla looked at Beatle as if she were focusing her camera lens on him, really zooming in, getting a sharp, clear picture of exactly what was going on. Beatle shoved his hands in his pockets and started walking towards home, figuring first you attack, then you turn your back and start moving so they can't see the whites of your eyes.

Cilla walked up behind him.

Toby, Magnus, Winsome, and Angie wisely kept some distance. It was typical Winsome to drop him right in it, then leave him to fend for himself.

"I'm serious, Beatle," Cilla said. "You've been weird all week. It's like you can't stand being near me, but then when you are, you buy me something as if you're madly in love with me, and it's messing with my head."

Beatle looked at her.

"As if I can't stand you? Weird all week? What are you talking about? That is absolute bullshit," he said, cranking up the volume. "What the fuck are you talking about? I've been really nice to you all week, and if buying a couple of things is freaking you out, then you can always hand them back. Well, not the Happy Meal and the Coke, but everything else . . ." and he did a "gimme" motion with his hands.

Cilla looked at him grimly.

"You didn't even touch me this weekend," she said quietly. "Not even a proper kiss."

"What? What are you talking about? I touched you. We kissed."

"A peck is different from a kiss. And when we were

alone, you kept talking; you were talking your head off, like you had all this stuff to say, but you didn't. You were just talking crap."

Beatle looked at her. Now he really was insulted. Talking crap?

"I'm sorry if I was trying to be interesting," he said, looking to the sky and shaking his head in the same way his mom did when she was trying to turn the screws and make him feel all guilty for hurting her feelings.

"You were trying to avoid me," Cilla insisted.

"How can I avoid you when you're over at my house every friggin' day?"

Cilla's face fell, as if her muscles couldn't keep her features in place any longer.

She turned away from him and started walking.

"I didn't mean it that way," he said gently, falling into step beside her. "I'm happy for you to be over. I love you coming 'round. I just meant, it's a bit rough for you to say I'm avoiding you when I'm spending tons of time with you."

They got to his block. Cilla kept walking. Beatle grabbed her and made her sit down on the low brick wall out front.

Toby, Magnus, and Angie walked on by with a "See ya" to Beatle and Cilla, and Winsome went inside. Ever the diplomat.

"Nothing's wrong," Beatle said, bending down to Cilla so they were eye-to-eye. "I just bought you some stuff to show you how great I think you are. The red roses were too much; I get that. I won't ever buy you flowers again. Cross my heart. Flowers are now officially off my list."

He tried a smile. She didn't respond.

"Come inside," he said, putting his hand on her elbow and trying to nudge her to her feet.

Cilla yanked her arm back and looked at him like he'd gone mad.

"What? You can't avoid me because I'm over at your house 'every friggin' day'—quote—and now you're asking me to come inside? You ever heard the term 'mixed messages,' 'cause you're some kind of Zen Jedi Master at it."

"Look," Beatle said, a sense of calmness flooding through him. He didn't want to be a bastard. Cilla was so sweet, so lovely, so cute. Look at her sitting there, with her hair pushed back by a red bobby pin and the ring he'd bought her in her nose and a frown pulling her eyebrows in. And her flowery dress and stripy stockings and red shoes—only Cilla could pull off a look like that. It was completely . . . weird, but it suited her. "I want you to come in," he said. "You have to anyway; Mum's done a chart for you, and she told me to get you to come by this afternoon and pick it up."

"I'm sure she can give it to me some other time," Cilla said coolly.

"Come on. Come inside. I feel like a bastard. You can't go home when I've been such a shit."

Cilla didn't seem prepared to budge, which wasn't like her. Usually Cilla was the most accommodating, yeah-whatever type girl you could ever meet. If they had a fight, Cilla would be the first to buckle. She'd be the one to start snuggling up to him, nestling into his back, trying to get him to smile. But this afternoon, she was pissed off and not wanting to move on from her pissed-off-ness.

"If you don't come in," Beatle added, upping the ante, "I'll keep buying you presents, and that'll really freak you out."

Cilla looked at him without a smile.

"I'll buy you a car, if you're not careful."

She sat there, not answering, not smiling, not responding, determined not to yield.

"Cilla, please," Beatle said, kneeling on the ground in front of her and sneaking a peek in under her lowered eyelashes. "Okay. No presents. Never again. Not even for your birthday. Not even for Christmas. Nothing. Ever again. Valentine's Day, forget it."

"You did forget it," she said. "It was on Saturday. No present."

"Oh," Beatle said, "that's true. But lucky, hey,

considering how annoying you find it when I give you something."

"See, that's the thing," Cilla said, staring down at her knees. "You don't get me anything for Valentine's Day, which is fine, I don't care, but then all this week it's like you're Mr. Generosity. It's weird."

As Beatle knelt in front of her, he noticed a safety pin on the path beside him. He knew what his mom would say: "See a pin and pick it up. All day long you'll have good luck." Beatle picked it up. Anything was worth a try. He looked back up into Cilla's face.

"Cill?"

He put the pin on her lap.

"See a pin and pick it up," he said. "All day long you'll have good luck."

She picked up the pin and twiddled it between her fingers.

"It's not a present, of course," Beatle warned. "It's just a little something. For you." He took her hand in his. "Please come inside," he said. "Please?"

And then finally, reluctantly, she said, "Oh god, okay. I'll come in. But only because I know your mum puts so much effort into her charts."

Beatle put his arms around her waist and dragged her close to him.

"I'm sorry," he said. "It's the whole senior-year thing.

Pressure. I don't know. But whatever it is, I shouldn't be taking it out on you."

Cilla looked across at him . . . and smiled. A sad kind of smile that seemed to be saying good-bye even as he came closer. He leaned over and kissed her on the mouth.

"Come on," he said, standing up and taking her hand. "Let's go and see what spooky astrological whatevers she's found in your chart."

Cilla followed him into their apartment.

"And I promise," he added as they stood on the threshold, "no presents. No asshole behavior."

And no kissing random girls, he added, but only inside his head.

*Y*our buddy is scraping the bottom of the boredom barrel by flipping through the local paper when she spots five lines of oddness among the standard singles ads in the classified section: "Stalker Wanted: Attractive twenty-something urban professional female seeks stalker for unsettling but nonthreatening harassment. Must be competent at leaving creepy phone messages and writing strange love notes. No time wasters!" and an e-mail address.

You:

a) E-mail for a joke, to see what kind of response you get.

b) Don't e-mail for a joke. Consider the dangers (remembering all the blah blah blah you've copped over the years from parents, teachers, and the newspapers about meeting strangers over the Internet) and decide it would be risky, stupid, and potentially hazardous to your health to send a return e-mail.

c) Don't even consider b) for a minute.

d) Not even for one second.

"It's a sign," Mathilde said, a wide-eyed look on her face to convey the significance of finding the "Stalker Wanted" ad. "I don't think I've ever read the local paper in my entire life. Ever. I don't think we even get it at our place. And the one time I read it, this crazy notice is the first thing I see. It's a sign. Fate. We have to reply."

Destiny, Netta, and Mathilde were all in the art room working on their projects. At least, Destiny and Netta were working on their projects. Mathilde was sitting with her feet propped on the desk, crossed at the ankles, ostentatiously ignoring the fact that she had an art project, which needed to be completed by the end of the year, and—according to Mr. Castles, their art teacher—she didn't have a clue about where she was going with it.

Mr. Castles was new to the school this year, and already the girls had figured out the following things about him: he was cool, he was super-talented, and he was working on a film project—a documentary—that he was hoping to have finished by the end of the year. As a matter of fact, the rumor was that he'd only agreed to come and teach at their school on the condition that he could use the multimedia edit suite whenever he liked.

"Maybe he should spend more time on *his* project and less time hassling me about where mine's going," Mathilde had grumbled this afternoon after Mr. Castles had thrown out most of her pieces and told her to start again.

Mr. Castles had called her work "too design-y by far" ("Whatever that means," Mathilde had said, with a disdainful click of her tongue), and "It needs to be pushed a lot further before you start getting anywhere," ("Probably off the nearest cliff," Mathilde had said), so she was serving him right by doing two-thirds of fuck-all.

Which had led to her finding the "Stalker Wanted" ad.

Netta was working on getting a hand exactly right. Netta could sit for hours and draw a single piece of anatomy until it was absolutely perfect; pencilling in and rubbing out a single finger or crease until you couldn't tell the difference between her drawing and the real thing. She could shade for hours, getting so involved in how the light fell that she didn't notice the sun going down on the real thing. There was no question she had talent. Of the three of them—really, of all the kids in their class— Netta was by far the most skilled at her craft and the most absorbed by her work. Sure, Destiny could sit for a while working on a piece, but then she'd have to get up and go to the bathroom, or get something to drink, or start yakking to someone. She'd get to the brink of absorption, and then she'd have to pull herself away because she didn't want to fall into the pit and miss anything that was going on around her. But not Netta. Often Netta would sneak down to the art room as if it were a guilty secret and work through her lunchtime making minor adjustments to a sketch, infinitesimally small changes that no one but she would notice. Working it and working it, but never—importantly—over-working it. Always having the foresight to know when something was finished and putting her brushes or pencils down.

While Netta worked on the knuckles of the hand she was sketching, Destiny was working on her canvas in the art room for the very sensible reason that she didn't want to get caught with Mrs. Sheffield's somewhat damaged, somewhat illegally stolen tapestry in her bedroom.

The night before, Mrs. Sheffield had come over to their place to give Destiny's mom the latest lowdown on what had happened when she tried to reclaim the tapestry from her ex-daughter-in-law, Susan.

"She denies taking it, of course. The police aren't going to do anything about it," she had said, chucking her chin towards the heavens. "Too busy selling corrupt drugs to their crooked friends to worry about innocent old ladies whose ex-daughters-in-law are nasty little thieves. I told them you'd seen her driving up and taking it," she'd said, looking over at Destiny, who'd swallowed, "but they said unless I had real proof, not just the say-so of some teenage girl, then there wasn't anything they could do."

"Um. I didn't actually say that I'd seen her take it,"

Destiny had pointed out. "In fact, I'm not even sure that the car stopped. Or that it was her car. We just saw this big car driving down the street. It could have been anyone."

Mrs. Sheffield had completely ignored her.

"It's probably in one of those pawn shops," she'd continued, taking a glug of the wine Destiny's mom had given her. "They'd get a lot of money for it, I'd wager. She," being Susan obviously, "wouldn't have a clue what it's worth. Although she knows who made it. Commented on it a number of times, she did."

Destiny's mom had tsk'ed in a noncommital way that had only seemed to encourage Mrs. Sheffield.

"But don't you worry," she'd said, wagging her finger, "I've got her number; I've got her tagged. She won't be able to get away with something like that again."

"No," Destiny's mom had said.

"I've got someone organized to keep an eye on the place. Watch out for her. She's not going to get away with it that easy. Antony, of course, went around to her place and told her she'd been seen taking it."

Destiny had gulped.

"They had a screaming match, apparently. She's nasty, that one. I told him not to marry her. She said she hadn't taken it, of course, and of course he didn't believe her. That's why I went to the police. To get a search warrant."

She had tipped more wine down her throat.

"What they do with their time, I've got no idea, but it certainly doesn't involve looking after the local community. I told them I was going to take it further. I've organized an appointment with Barry Shoeman next week, to tell him what's been going on."

"Who's Barry Shoeman?" Destiny had asked.

"Our local member of parliament," her mom had answered.

"Oh."

So yeah, Destiny had figured it would be best if she worked on her art at school, at least until she'd finished her piece with the tapestry.

"I'm gonna reply," Mathilde said, swinging her feet onto the floor. "And you know what? This could be my theme. For my project. Stalking. I could take photos of us stalking this girl. It could be really cool. The whole thing about watching someone. Getting them unsettled. Whaddya think? It could be good."

"That ad can't be serious," Netta said, momentarily flicking her eyes up from her page, then focusing back on the sketch she was doing of Mathilde's hand. (Which had given Mathilde another reason not to work on her project—"Busy. Posing.") "As if you'd advertise for a stalker. It must be a joke. Or some kind of code. You know, 'Buy drugs here' or 'Party at my place tonight.' That type of thing."

Destiny looked up from her canvas. The tapestry was glued down onto the left-hand side of the frame, and she was now stitching around the edges with fluorescent orange thread. Who'd have thought sewing lessons in junior high would come in so handy?

"I'll bet it's for real," Destiny said. "Remember that guy in Germany who advertised for someone to eat? That cannibal guy?"

"Hannibal Lecter?" Mathilde asked.

Destiny shook her head.

"That wasn't a true story, you know," Mathilde continued. "It's what they call fic-tion. Made-up stories. They're not real."

Destiny rolled her eyes at Mathilde. If there was a smart-ass comment to be made, or a smart-ass way to say it, Mathilde was always willing to step up to the plate.

"This wasn't fiction. This guy was for real," Destiny said. "Ern couldn't stop reading about him."

Her brother Ernest—being the fifteen-year-old boy that he was—took very seriously his role of being gross, smelly, and revolting. Reading about cannibals advertising for someone to eat was gross and revolting, and something Ern had taken to with relish. Tomato relish, some would say.

"What happened was," Destiny went on, "this guy advertised on the Internet for someone to eat. And some other guy replied, saying he'd like to be eaten. So the first guy ate the second guy—like, he actually ate him. Dead. And then he had to go to court for murder. I can't believe you didn't hear about it."

Netta and Mathilde were both staring at her.

"I can't remember what happened to him," Destiny added. It wasn't often Mathilde was lost for words, so Destiny took full advantage. "I think it was all a bit funny, because the dead guy had said he wanted to be eaten. Which meant, he was happy to die, obviously. And also, because cannibalism isn't a crime in Germany, it was all a bit dodgy. And the other weird thing about it—"

"What? There's more weird stuff about it?" asked Mathilde.

"—was he got about seven replies from people saying they wanted to be eaten, too. And some of them he didn't choose because they weren't the right build—didn't look tasty enough, I suppose—and a couple of others freaked out when it got close to dinnertime. But this one guy went ahead with it. So yeah, people advertise for some pretty weird things."

Netta shook her head and turned back to her paper, her pencil moving carefully on the page.

"But you wouldn't want a stalker," Netta said. "A friend of Mum's has been stalked, and it's really bad what's happened to her. This guy's set her yard on fire, he lets out her tires all the time, he leaves flyers in her neighbors' mailboxes saying she's operating a brothel."

Mathilde laughed. "Omigod. Is she?"

Netta frowned.

"As if. She's one of Mum's friends. He's just decided he's going to make her life hell. I can't believe someone would advertise for something like that."

"What's weirder—" asked Mathilde, "someone advertising for a stalker or advertising for someone to eat?"

The three girls sat quietly for a moment.

"Hmm," said Destiny finally. "The stalker is definitely more normal. She obviously just wants to make her boyfriend jealous or something."

"Yeah, stalking," Netta agreed begrudgingly.

"I'm gonna reply," Mathilde said. "Do her a favor. I mean, if I was going to have someone stalking me, I'd rather it was us than some crazy person."

Destiny thought about it, then nodded. "Definitely. I mean, of all the stalkers in the world, we'd probably be the nicest."

"And most normal," added Mathilde. "I mean, we certainly wouldn't set anything on fire."

"Or let out tires," added Destiny.

"No," agreed Mathilde. "Don't know how to."

"I think you put a pin into the nozzle that you put the air in or something," said Destiny.

"Sounds too much like hard work," said Mathilde, shaking her head. "A flyer to the neighbors would be quite funny, though."

"Yeah," said Destiny.

"And could be a nice touch. You know, threatening without being dangerous."

"Yeah."

Netta frowned at her two friends.

"You're not," she said.

"Not what?"

"Not replying."

"Yeah. Why wouldn't we?" asked Mathilde.

"I'm not even going to continue this conversation," said Netta, "because I know you wouldn't be so stupid."

"*Au contraire*," said Mathilde. "You have no idea how stupid we can be."

"Yeah yeah yeah," said Netta in a bored voice as she went back to her sketching. "You don't think I've seen you both at your stupid-worst? I've seen it all, but even you guys wouldn't be so stupid as to e-mail some psychonutcase and apply for a job as resident stalker."

Mathilde and Destiny looked at each other.

"Whaddya think?" said Mathilde.

"Stupid if we don't," said Destiny.

"Besides," said Mathilde, "we're just doing it out of curiosity. And for my project. It could be kind of bizarre and fun. Different stalking situations. Take some photos. Clip out this ad and put it on the canvas. Maybe do some computer stuff with it. Famous stalkers of our time."

"Omigod," said Destiny. "That's a brilliant idea. It could be really cool."

Netta shook her head again.

"Don't. I mean, sure, use it in your project, but don't e-mail her. You don't know who she is."

"We'll just write once," said Mathilde. "See what she says. Satisfy our curiosity. Chill," she said to Netta. "It'll be fine."

There's just one thing about curiosity—rumor has it that it kills.

To: ange398@hotmail.com.au
From: waltzingmathilde@hotmail.com.au
Date: February 18
Subject: Stalker ad
Dear ange398,

Saw your ad in the local paper, and thought we might apply. We don't really have any qualifications for this type of position. However, we are extremely motivated and feel that what we lack in experience, we make up for in general enthusiasm.

We noticed in your ad that you said you were a woman and this could be the only hitch with our application—we are also female. Do you have a problem with that? There are three of us, and depending on where you live, we feel we can commit to one or two nights of stalking per week.

Please let us know as soon as possible whether you would like us for the role.

Yours faithfully,
Mathilde, Netta, and Destiny
PS Is this a paying position?

To: waltzingmathilde@hotmail.com.au
From: ange398@hotmail.com.au
Date: February 18
Subject: Re: Stalker ad
Dear Mathilde, Netta, and Destiny,

Thank you for your prompt reply.

The role of stalker is gender-neutral.

My address is 38 Mackie Avenue, East St Kilda. Perhaps we could try a sample piece of stalking tomorrow night at around 6 p.m.

Looking forward to it.
Ange

*T*wo identical old-lady twins appear on the screen. "Martha" and "Joan." Both of them have blue hair.

"Everyone did their bit during the war," Martha says. "No one bought new clothes. If something had a hole in it, you patched it. You didn't throw it out." Her twin nods slowly. "We were only young, mind, sixteen when it started, but we were very conscious of not being wasteful. Of making a contribution to the war effort."

Joan moves in her chair, shifting so that she can watch her sister talk instead of facing the camera.

"We were eighteen when we met a lovely young man. Bill," says Martha, a shy smile warming her face. "He was gorgeous. Good fun. We'd go to dances together, and he'd always take the two of us," she nods towards her twin, "but it was me that he was interested in, wasn't it?" she asks her twin, knocking her arm gently with the back of her hand.

Joan nods, smiling. "Oh yes," she agrees. "He was mad about her. Absolutely mad."

"After a short time he asked me to marry him. He was about to be sent off, and he told me he wanted to marry me as soon as he came back. He wanted me to wait for him."

Martha looks straight up at the camera.

"I mean, that was the sort of thing you did in those days—you can't imagine it, I suppose. If you met someone and you loved them, you promised you would wait for them. Even though you knew, well, we knew there was a chance he might not come back."

"In the meantime, I got a job decoding messages at the army barracks on St Kilda Road," Joan interrupts, taking up the narrative. "I'd sit at my desk each day and decode all sorts of things. Whatever landed on my desk, I'd have to decode."

She looks up at the camera.

"Actually, it was rather dull a lot of the time. Messages about this and that. A lot of it about troop movements, boat coordinates, that type of thing."

Her twin sister resumes her side of the story:

"So Bill was away, and we knew where he was stationed, and he wrote to me as regularly as he could. Sometimes I'd get three and four letters in one go, and then nothing for a few weeks. But he was a good letter-writer, wasn't he?" Joan nods. "And over the months, he kept writing and seemed to keep missing the action.

Finally, he wrote a letter telling me that he was on his way home for a short while, and we should get married while he was on leave."

She smiles to herself, her hands folded like an origami bird in the nest of her lap.

Joan starts talking again:

"So Martha got things organized. It didn't take a lot of preparation really, did it? It was going to be a simple wedding, a few friends and family. Martha and I made the wedding dress, and it was absolutely stunning. Stunning. Plain white cotton. We couldn't really get anything fancier, because fabrics were so expensive in those days, but we spent every night madly embroidering it, so that it would be ready in time for Bill's return. And we knew what ship he was on, and when he was due home. Then, one day I was at work and a message came through that the ship he was on had been bombed. There were no survivors. I mean, it was a complete coincidence that I got the message. It could have gone to any one of us—there were about fifty people working there. But I got it. I decoded it. And I knew instantly that Bill was dead."

Martha sits there, watching her twin talk.

"But I couldn't say anything," Joan says quietly. "Because I wasn't allowed to. It was confidential. I wasn't allowed to speak about my work to anyone. Not even my sister. So I couldn't tell her. I had to wait for her to receive the telegram. Meanwhile, each night, we were embroidering her wedding dress, me knowing that there was not going to be a wedding."

She looks up at the camera again.

"But that's how it was. That's how things went, in those days."

"Ooh," said his mom, as soon as she saw the roses, "that's bad luck."

"Roses?" said Beatle. As if he wanted to talk even more about the damn roses. "I don't think so. I think you'll find they're considered romantic."

Enough said.

"Not with those thorns, they're not," his mom said, tilting her chin in the direction of the flowers. "You never want to give roses with thorns. It's bad luck."

"And a sign of a guilty conscience," Winsome added, once more for luck.

Beatle looked irritably at his mom. And Winsome.

"Jesus. I buy flowers, and all I've got is shit for it. Seriously, that's the last time."

"Are they from down the road?" his mom asked, tossing her head in the general direction of down the road.

Cilla nodded.

Beatle's mom started plucking the thorns off with her fingers. "They're hopeless there," she said. "You'd think they'd know. No thorns on red roses. I mean honestly, how hard can it be? It's not rocket science. They're probably selling knives as gifts, too."

"I don't think so," Cilla said. "It's a flower shop."

"Oh, I know, darling. I'm just saying, if they sell roses with thorns, they'd do anything."

Cilla had been going out with Beatle for three years now, but she still didn't seem to get how much of a space cadet his mom was. Beatle found the best way to deal with his mom was to say, "Uh-huh," and be done with it. But Cilla wasn't like that.

"What's the problem with giving a knife as a gift?" she asked. Prodding. Probing. Keeping the conversation going. Long after its expiration date.

Beatle sighed. He could have told her. Give knives as a gift, and you'll be severing ties with your friend before long.

". . . severing ties with your friend before long. Same with scissors, swords, and letter openers," his mom went on.

"Because people regularly give swords and letter openers as gifts," put in Winsome as she opened the fridge door.

"Watches and clocks are another one," his mom added, ignoring the sarcasm coming from the fridge. "They don't sever, but they do symbolize a limited life span, which is hardly a great gift to give a friend."

Beatle watched his mom yabbering on about what you could and couldn't give and why. And what for. And who gives a shit anyway?

"And you never give an empty wallet or purse," she continued. "That's bad luck, too. Says they'll always lack money. Always put a couple of coins in it. And if you are given an empty wallet or purse, get rid of it. Give it to a friend—but put some coins in it so they get good luck. What else is there?" she said, to the ceiling. "Handkerchiefs are another no-no. They mean the person you're giving them to is going to be crying a lot."

"Gawd," said Cilla. "I had no idea finding a present for a friend was so difficult."

"Oh it is, darling. It's absolutely perilous."

Cilla grinned. "So, Beatle told me you've got a little something for me," she said, raising an eyebrow.

Beatle's mom smiled.

"That I do," she said, wiping a crumb off her lap. More of a nervous thing than an actual cleaning-up thing. Beatle should know—his mom never cleaned.

Never cooked, never shopped.

Too busy sitting at her computer doing star charts for her customers.

And—unfortunately for her children—star charts for her children.

And for her children's girlfriends and boyfriends.

"So," Cilla said, settling herself down at the kitchen table. "What's this year got in store for me? Should I spend it at home hiding under my bed?"

Beatle's mom stood up and reached over to pick up the folder marked "Cilla" on the kitchen bench.

"Oh, there won't be any hiding under the bed," his mom said, swatting Cilla's ridiculous notion away with her hand, "but it is a year of great change."

"Being senior year and all," Winsome said, "I suppose it is."

Mrs. Lennon smiled, then settled her ample behind comfortably into a chair and smoothed out the chart she'd printed off her computer. It was full of dots and swipes and markings that Beatle didn't have a clue about, and as they sat there—with Cilla pointing at this or that and asking questions—he had the feeling of being trapped.

Sometimes it was like Cilla was more friendly with his mom and his sister than she was with him. Like she was a member of the family, even though she wasn't. Like they were married already, even though they were only eighteen. Cilla would sit around and joke with his mom and whisper secrets with his sister, and sometimes it gave him this bad feeling in his stomach. Admittedly she'd been Winsome's best friend since the beginning of high school, so she was pretty much in the family, but when she'd act really friendly-shmiendly, Beatle would get washed over with the feeling that he was locked into this relationship with her, and there was no way out.

Sometimes he thought of her as his "accidental girl-friend." They'd only started going out with each other because he'd had a stroke. They'd only kissed because she'd come in to see him in the hospital when he was having a rough day. The opportunity had only arisen because she was his sister's best friend. Their relation-ship hadn't been a choice thing; it had been more of a circumstantial thing. That's not to say he wasn't happy with her. He was. Once he'd kissed her, once they'd kissed a few times, he was mad about her. But that didn't stop him from wondering whether it was an accident that they were together.

And then there was this fling-thing he'd had with Destiny. That had to mean something.

His mind kept circling the question, picking over it like a vulture. Vultures only picked at dead things, didn't they? Or nearly dead things. Was his relationship with Cilla dead? Or dying?

The tricky thing was, how do you turn around and drop your sister's best friend?

He looked over at his mom and Cilla poring over the star chart, laughing at something his mom was carrying on about.

Beatle left the kitchen and went into his bedroom to do some homework.

Cilla came in a little later to say good-bye.

He pretended not to hear the door to his bedroom opening. As if he were engrossed by the math problems he was working out. Cilla came up behind him and put her hands on his shoulders and slid them down his body to his waist. She kissed his ear.

"You did it again," she said softly. He almost wasn't sure she'd said it.

"Did what?" he asked, turning around so she had to step back.

"Left me on my own. Invited me in, then left me on my own with your mum."

"I'm studying," he said carefully, not letting the irritation into his voice. "I've got a test. I couldn't sit around the kitchen all afternoon listening to Mum and her crazy predictions."

"But I could?" Cilla said.

Beatle sighed.

"No, probably not. What did she say, anyway?" he asked.

"She said there's going to be big changes. Things are going to be a lot different next year."

"Gee. Thanks, Captain Obvious. Lucky you didn't pay good money for that."

"Hmm. Lucky," Cilla agreed.

But she didn't sound like someone who was basking in the warm glow of Lady Luck's attention at that particular moment.

*D*estiny, Mathilde, and Netta caught the No. 16 tram down to Mackie Avenue, East St Kilda.

Just as a matter of interest, the No. 16 tram used to be the No. 69, a fact which every self-respecting teenager had found well worth a giggle. But presumably the Tramways Board discovered that school kids were sniggering to themselves all the way along the 69 tram route and put an end to the whole sordid business.

"So let me get this straight," Destiny's dad had said when he found out about the renumbering. "The trams run late, are overcrowded, and security is a problem. But instead of adding more trams or bringing back conductors, the Tramways Board run their eye down their to-do list, figure everything else is too hard, renumber the sixty-nine tram sixteen and dust off their hands, feeling that there's a job well done. Brilliant. Absolutely brilliant. Bureaucracy at its best."

The No. 16 tram goes from Cotham Road in Kew, along Glenferrie Road, twists down Hawthorn Road, turns right into Balaclava Road which changes into Carlisle Street, past Luna Park in St Kilda through West St Kilda and Middle Park and Albert Park into the city and stops at Carlton. (This description of the tram route is so accurate, you can use this book as your official travel guide to Melbourne next time you're in town.)

So Destiny, Mathilde, and Netta were on the 69 tram—renumbered 16—travelling down to their first-ever official stalking engagement on Mackie Avenue, East St Kilda. Destiny wearing a khaki T-shirt and army fatigues, Mathilde wearing a pair of jeans and black T-shirt, and Netta in a skirt with a green-and-pink striped top and jangly bracelet. . . .

"Your outfit just needs one last thing to finish it off," Destiny said, when Netta arrived at the tram stop at the designated time of 1600 hours (also known as 4 p.m.).

"What?" asked Netta.

"A flashing neon sign that says 'look at me'?" suggested Mathilde.

"Exactly," said Destiny.

"You want me to come along, you deal with my choice of outfit," Netta huffed.

Destiny didn't care about Netta's outfit as much as she cared about the fact that Beatle hadn't called.

"It's the fifth day, you know," she pointed out.

Mathilde chewed her lip.

"Not a good sign," Destiny continued.

Destiny, Mathilde, and Netta had a sliding scale that they found useful when gauging a boy's interest.

If he called the day immediately after a date, he was interested. Very interested. Maybe even too interested.

Calling the day immediately after indicated possible psycho tendencies. Warning bells should ring. It's not that you wouldn't go out with him, but you would definitely be on alert, checking him out for evidence of other psycho behavior: whether he gets irritable easily; if he tells stories about ex-girlfriends that may demonstrate bad behavior on his part; that type of thing.

The day after that—the second day—showed that he was interested, but not too interested. Not psycho interested. The second day was probably the optimum day for a guy to call.

The day after that—day number three—was still good. It showed he was reasonably interested, but not desperate or psychopathically inclined.

Day four was begrudgingly acceptable but teetering on disinterested.

Day five was considered a tipping point. Maybe he liked you, but not enough to get on the phone with any great urgency. Destiny, Mathilde, and Netta had decided that a lapse of five days showed a lazy attitude, which is not something you'd be altogether happy with in a relationship.

And after that . . . six days. Well, that was plain insulting. They'd decided the sixth day should be called the accidental day, because it was like he hadn't even considered calling you for even a moment, and then, for some reason, he finds your phone number—accidentally—it's not like he's looking for it or anything; maybe he puts on the pants he wore that night and finds the number in his pocket; maybe he pulls it out of his wallet when he's searching for some cash—whatever—and seeing the number thinks, "Maybe I'll give her a call," but really, it's a completely accidental thing.

And today was the fifth day since Destiny had chowed down on Subway with Beatle at the botanical gardens.

The tipping point.

"I mean, seriously," Destiny said as the tram trundled over the intersection of Glenferrie and Dandenong roads and did a dog-leg down Hawthorn, "we got on really well, had lots of fun, good laughs, and then he doesn't call. Go figure."

Mathilde and Netta shook their heads.

"Maybe he doesn't want to get involved in his senior year," suggested Netta.

"That's a pretty lame reason not to call," Destiny said glumly.

"Maybe it's something to do with his limp," said Mathilde, clicking her fingers as the idea sprang into her head. "Remember you said he limped? Maybe something bad happened to him with a girl, and that's how he got the limp, and now he's vowed never to get close to a girl again."

"That's kind of romantic," Netta said.

"Very," decided Mathilde.

But Destiny shook her head.

"Nuh. That's not it. And you know what the worst part is?"

"I thought the worst part was that he hadn't called," said Mathilde.

"The worst thing is," said Destiny, ignoring her friend, "giving your phone number to a boy—your real phone number—is a trust thing. It says, 'I like you enough to trust you with my phone number. I trust you will use it for good, not evil. That you will use it to call, not *not*-call.' You know what I mean? And the fact that he hasn't called is kind of more insulting than if he hadn't asked for my number in the first place."

Which reminded Destiny of Henry Muscamp, the boy she'd recently given a fake phone number to. The boy she'd accidentally kissed at Meredith's party, because she was drunk and he was persistent. She'd considered herself lucky to have the presence of mind to give him a fake number when he'd blindsided her by asking if he could call her and maybe go out, but now she was thinking about how it must have felt for Henry when he'd called her—which she felt sure he had. And he must have gotten either an operator's patient recorded voice telling him that the number was not connected or some stranger answered the phone and said, "Destiny? No, you must have the wrong number," and then Henry would have double-checked and said, "Is this blah blah blah blah blah whatever-number-she'd-given-him," and the person on the other end would have said, "Yeah, you've called the right number, but there's no Destiny here." And then Henry must have known that she'd given him a fake number, and he may or may not have told his friends, depending on how far he wanted his red-faced embarrassment to spread. But now, sitting on the tram wondering why Beatle hadn't called, Destiny thought it was probably a pretty mean trick to have played on poor old Henry Muscamp.

"Maybe he's not calling because he's from the wrong side of the tracks," Mathilde said, clicking her fingers again to signify a new idea had entered her brain. "You know, you're from Kew, he's from East St Kilda. It's classic wrong-side-of-the-tracks stuff. Happens all the time."

"All the time," agreed Netta. "Movies are full of it."

"You two are full of it," Destiny said.

And then there was that other poor guy, Simon Whitfield, who Mathilde had a bit of a fling with. When

Mathilde had gotten sick of him, she'd complained to Destiny that whenever he called she didn't want to speak to him, but she felt obliged to answer the phone, anyway. So Destiny had come up with the brainwave—absolute unadulterated brainwave—of changing his name in Mathilde's contact list to "Don't answer," so every time poor old Simon Whitfield tried to call, his number came up on Mathilde's phone as "Don't answer," so Mathilde didn't. Instead of saying to the poor guy, "Listen, I think you're really nice, but I'm not that into you. Nothing personal," Mathilde had ignored his calls until he'd gotten the hint.

"Maybe it's God paying me back for all the mean things I've done," Destiny wondered out loud.

"I know what's happened," Mathilde said, clicking her fingers yet again. "He's had a terrible accident and can't call because he's broken his hand."

Destiny stared at her friend for a moment.

"He could use his other one," Destiny said finally, the cool, rational voice of the hurt woman who doesn't want to relinquish the hurt just yet.

"He broke both hands," suggested Netta.

Destiny looked at Netta. "He could get his sister to call."

"Maybe her hands broke in the same accident," decided Mathilde.

"Absolutely," said Netta. "That's definitely what happened."

"He could get his mum to call," said Destiny.

"She can't," said Mathilde.

"Both hands," Netta held up both her own hands to demonstrate, "broken."

Destiny rolled her eyes.

"He could use his feet," she said.

"Broken," said Mathilde.

"His nose," Destiny said.

"He can dial a phone with his nose?" Netta asked. "I hadn't noticed it was that pointy."

"It's pointy enough," Destiny said with a smirk.

"Gosh, no wonder you want him to call," Mathilde said.

And the three of them burst out laughing.

"Maybe *you* should call him," said Netta at last. "You know, see if he wants to do something."

"I can't. You know I don't do that kind of thing. I'd be too shy. Besides, if he's not that interested, there's not much point, is there?"

"Yeah. S'pose."

Mathilde clicked her fingers at her friends. Not because another idea had entered her head, but because the tram had turned down Balaclava Road, and Mackie Avenue was a couple of streets up.

"This is it," she said, standing up.

They got off the tram and started walking towards their stalking assignment.

"Besides," Destiny added as they headed along Mackie Avenue, past the '70s brown-brick block of apartments on the corner, "I don't have his phone number."

"You could get it off Frank," said Mathilde as they passed a house with a rusted car in the front yard. "He's his teacher. It'd be in the school records."

"As if," Destiny said, kicking at a stone on the path. "Imagine what he'd say. I've heard enough 'Destiny and whoever, sitting in a tree' from him to last me a lifetime. You know what he's like. He's so juvenile. Imagine asking him for one of his student's phone numbers. He'd never let me forget it."

Mathilde stopped.

"This is it," she said, looking at the house of their victim.

Number 38 Mackie Avenue, East St Kilda.

A weatherboard house with peeling paint and no pretty details at all. Just some spindly bushes in the front. A house that looked a bit sinister actually, maybe the kind of thing Boo Radley would live in if he'd moved from 1930s America to current-day East St Kilda.

"Hmm," said Destiny.

"I'm still not sure about this," said Netta.

"Don't worry about it," said Mathilde. "It'll be fine. We won't even speak to her. If you don't want to come again, you don't have to. But you've gotta admit you're curious."

Netta shrugged. "A little."

"So how do we do this?" asked Destiny. "Just sit out in front here?"

Mathilde chewed her lip and looked around.

"I think that would be a bit weird. And not very stalkerish, I imagine. I'm sure you're supposed to stay hidden so they don't see you. Don't you think? Maybe we should go and hide in the garden across the road."

Destiny shook her head.

"I'm not hiding in someone's garden. We might get arrested. Or murdered," she added, looking at the house across the road.

"Well, what do you suggest?"

"I don't know. How about we sit on the curb on the other side and act like we're stalking someone?"

"Which we are, ironically," Netta pointed out.

"Yeah. So it's the perfect disguise," Destiny said, grinning.

"Okay. Perfect," said Mathilde, pulling out her camera. "I'll take a couple of shots of you guys looking stalkerish while we're waiting. For my project."

While Destiny and Netta sat in the gutter and stalked the house, Mathilde took some shots. It was getting close to 5:30 p.m., but even though Melbourne's summer was nearly at an end, the day was still bright.

"Did Emily tell you what happened to her last night?" Mathilde asked.

"No," they both answered.

Emily Bradshaw's Valentine's Day party had started off with just a few friends coming over (Destiny, Netta, and Mathilde) because her parents were away for the weekend, but of course, it had gotten a little bigger than that—as all parties without parents (or PWPs) seem to.

PWPs follow a similar principle to pyramid schemes, Mathilde maintained. You've got your person whose parents aren't home at the tip of the pyramid—in this case, Emily. So Emily calls a few friends—the next tier of the pyramid down. And then those few friends call a few friends—the next tier down. And so on and so forth, with the number of people growing each time someone on the next tier down calls a friend, causing a trickle effect which then becomes a cascade which then becomes a flood once the number becomes large enough.

Emily's party had gone past being a flood to something that would have had Noah reaching for his ark-building materials pronto. At one point in the night Destiny had leaned back against the kitchen bench and looked around. The house was a heaving mass of bodies. Beth was over in a corner crying while Bella put an arm around her and comforted her. Nina had cracked into sobs as well, probably because Christian had gone upstairs with Mirella, who was a known slut (probably the reason Christian had gone upstairs with her). Emily had come through the kitchen with her arm around Justin, who looked like he was about to vomit—interesting to see how quickly everyone got out of the way when they saw him coming through. Hattie was kissing some guy Destiny had never seen before. Fiona was laughing as loudly as she could to show how much fun she was—a tactic she often employed at parties. A couple of guys were up on the pool table playing air guitar for no one in particular.

Yep, that had sure been one helluva good party.

They'd all heard at school on Monday morning about the severe punishment that Emily's parents had meted out, including making her pay for repairs to the pool table, which had surprisingly collapsed. It was going to cost about a thousand dollars to fix. Where Emily was going to get a thousand bucks from was beyond them, but Mathilde had suggested they put on a fund-raiser—"You know, like what they do for blind kids"—to help raise the money.

"Well, last night," Mathilde said, watching Destiny and Netta through her camera, "her dad took the vodka out of the freezer to make a drink. But," she clicked the shutter, and then moved and squatted down to get a better angle, "when he went to pour it, it just stayed in the bottom of the bottle, frozen solid. So he said to Emily, 'How do you think this got frozen?' and Emily said to him, 'Well, you put it in the freezer. What did you expect?' and then he said, 'Vodka doesn't freeze.'"

Destiny and Netta stared at Mathilde blankly.

"People at the party had drunk the vodka," said Mathilde, taking the camera away from her face and letting it hang from the straps as if she were a professional photo-journalist, "so Emily had filled it up with water, figuring her folks wouldn't notice. She has to be the only person at school whose parents keep their vodka in the freezer. So then her dad went through all his bottles and found they'd all been filled up with either water or black tea."

"Black tea?" asked Netta.

"Yeah. You know, because it looks like scotch. Or brandy. Or whatever. So now Emily's in trouble all over again because her dad has to buy all these new drinks to replace the ones people drank at the party."

A man came walking up to the three girls. Quite handsome, but old, maybe thirty, thirty-five.

"Are you all right?" he asked.

"Yeah," said Mathilde. "You?"

"What are you doing?" he asked, ignoring her smart-ass-ism.

"Just taking some photos," said Netta.

"Waiting for a friend of ours," said Destiny.

"Who?" he asked.

"Um, Ange. She lives across the road," said Netta.

"I don't think so," he said. "An old guy lives there. Nick. He's lived there for years."

But then he nodded as if he'd just remembered something.

"You don't mean Angelo, do you? The son?"

"Angelo?" asked Destiny, a sick, creepy feeling sliding down her back. "Um. No. This is a girl, definitely. Called Ange."

"Yeah. Ange. Angelo," said the guy.

"No. We're waiting for a girl," insisted Mathilde.

"Right. Well, must be a coincidence then," said the guy, shrugging. "I wouldn't be hanging around the front of their place, though, if I was you. Angelo's not the friendliest of guys. Always off his head about something or other. You wouldn't want him to catch you staring at his joint. Who knows what he'd do?"

And then the guy walked away, leaving the three girls staring at the weatherboard house with its peeling paint and spindly bushes and general overall sinister feel.

A very attractive girl in her early twenties sits on a chair by herself. An empty chair is beside her, as if her other half is missing.

She sighs and looks up at the camera.

"I mean, I assume most people have read about us. That's why you got me in, isn't it?" she says directly to the camera. "It's been in the papers. And then there was that stupid story they did on *Today in Melbourne*. So probably everyone knows, yeah."

An indistinct mumble answers her.

"I'm glad," she goes on, biting a fingernail, "to be able to get my side of the story straight. I mean, everyone thinks I'm being a bitch, but I'm not. Just because she's my twin doesn't mean I should lie down and let her get away with it. That title was worth a lot of money. Who knows what other job opportunities would have come out of it for me if I'd won?"

The interviewer mumbles something else.

The girl shakes her pretty head adamantly.

"Hello?" she says. "It's a beauty contest. People win because of how they look. And I would have looked like her if I'd worn that dress. Or put it this way: she won because she looked the way I was going to look if I'd bought that dress."

She pushes her hair off her face and wipes her hand over her eyes, tension settling into her shoulders.

"I saw it first. I tried it on. I had them put it away for me. And when Sophie walked into the shop and the girl brought it out from the back for her to try on 'again,' Sophie knew instantly it was mine. *As if* she didn't know. The shop girl was an idiot bringing it out without checking first, but Sophie knew it was mine as soon as the girl brought it out."

The interviewer asks another question. The girl narrows her eyes and shakes her head angrily.

"No. I don't agree. I think stealing my dress is extreme. I think stealing the crown I should have won is extreme. I don't think suing my twin is extreme. She needs to be taught a lesson. You don't understand. She's always been like this. Always got her own way. Always."

She listens as the interviewer talks, then folds her arms across her chest.

"Well, I don't know," she says, tossing her head. "We'll see on Christmas Day, I suppose. All I know is, I'm not going for lunch at their place if she's there. It's up to Mum and Dad. Their choice. Me or her."

She shrugs.

"Simple."

And she looks defiantly at the camera as if challenging someone to a fight.

*B*eatle went into the kitchen to get something to eat.

"Where have you been, love?" his mom asked, hair floofed up, a kaftan-ish dress on her substantial frame, and large chandelier earrings glinting—all ready for bingo.

"Just studying," he said.

"You're a good boy," said his aunt Lally, smiling at him but neglecting to take the cigarette out of her mouth, so she could only smile with half a mouth.

Lally, who lived in the apartment upstairs, and Jools, who lived nearby, sat at the kitchen table, cigarettes in mouth, lipstick bleeding into the smoking creases they'd both nurtured around their lips over the years.

"I thought you would have gone with Winsome," Beatle's mom said.

"Where?"

"She's gone to meet Cilla somewhere. You didn't want to go?"

Beatle shrugged. "She didn't ask me."

His mom looked down at her fingernails, as if they were very interesting—which they were, painted with different flags from her favorite countries—then looked back up at Beatle.

"Is everything all right with you two?" she asked.

"With Winsome?"

"No. You and Cilla."

Lally and Jools pricked up their ears. Lally stubbed out her cigarette and pulled a fresh one out of the packet, ready to settle in for an episode of *Dramas of the Young and Eighteen*. Jools hooked her claw around the bottle they were drinking from and tipped more wine into the three glasses on the table. Beatle's mom put her hand over her glass.

"Oh, no more for me, thanks," she said, acting as if responsible drinking was her thing.

"A splash more," said Jools, squirting into the glass as Beatle's mom took her hand away. Then Jools said to Beatle, "So, getting back to the matter at hand, trouble in paradise? You and Cilla going through a hard time?"

Beatle glared at Jools. What did she think? Of all the people in all the world, she was the one he was going to confide in?

"No. Everything's fine," he said.

"I told you I saw some stuff in your chart last week," his mom said, tapping her fingernail on the table. "And

Cilla's chart points to a lot of changes. And then, the thorns on the roses . . . Sometimes it helps to talk about things."

Beatle looked at his mom. At Lally. At Jools. Was his mom completely and utterly insane? Did she honestly think he'd consider confiding in the three of them?

He had four words for her: I. Don't. Think. So.

"No. It's fine," he said, his teeth clamped.

"Okay. Well, you know you can talk if you want," his mom said.

And then she picked up her cigarette pack and tapped it on the table. She flipped open the lid, counted how many were left, and turned back to Beatle.

"Darling," she said, pouting her mouth at him, "I've only got a couple of ciggies left. Can you go up the street for me?"

Beatle waited a moment.

"And we've run out of milk," she added. "Be a love."

And then she thought some more.

"And some bread. Can you grab a loaf?"

"What did your last servant die of?" he asked.

His mom grinned.

"Boredom—I didn't give him enough to do. That's why there's only you and your sister left. I used to have three servants. I mean, children."

Lally and Jools laughed, and Beatle's mom looked

well pleased with her lame joke. Beatle sighed. "You're on fire," he said.

Lally licked her finger, then leaned over to prod Beatle's mom in the shoulder with an accompanying *sss* as if she were a hot coal.

"So ciggies, milk, and bread?" he asked.

"Grab some bread for me as well, thanks, Beat," said Jools.

"Ditto," said Lally.

A few years ago, Beatle would have told them all to get stuffed.

A few years ago, Beatle had been your standard fifteen-year-old with attitude (he'd never had as much attitude as Winsome, but who did?) and he would only run up the street for them if they paid him. But after his stroke, the way he felt about his mom had changed. Before his stroke, he'd found her embarrassing. She told bad jokes. She was stupidly superstitious. She'd chat to his friends and talk too loudly and drink too much too early in the day. She didn't cook. The house was a pigsty. She had no sense of modesty. Once, walking back to the car after they'd been swimming at Elwood Beach, the outline of her prominent droopy boobs was visible through her soaking wet T-shirt, and he had felt a fury well up inside him because she didn't even have the good grace to fold her arms across her chest to conceal them. Other times, he'd go into the bathroom to brush his teeth, and she'd be in the shower with no clothes on, and it disgusted him that she'd stand there naked in front of him. He remembered saying to her once, "Do you mind?" and she'd laughed and said, "Well, I'm in the shower—what do you expect?" as if it were perfectly normal to stand bare-butt naked in front of your own son.

But after his stroke, he'd gotten a bit more perspective. It's not that he wasn't embarrassed by her regularly—nearly every day—but he didn't care as much. He was a bit more "live and let live," as opposed to the traditional teen attitude of "live and wish everyone else in your family would disappear."

"Maybe you should do a reading," Lally suggested as Beatle started rummaging through his mom's bag for some money. "See how the night's going to pan out."

"That's a brilliant idea," said Beatle's mom, clicking her fingers at him. "Grab my cards for me, will you, darling? While you're there."

He tossed her the tarot cards on the bench, then left the kitchen as fast as his limping leg would carry him. He knew that being in the same room as tarot cards when they were dealt could lead to anything. And today, he didn't want to go there.

He decided to go down to the market on Carlisle Street, rather than to the 7-Eleven on the corner. It took longer to get there, but with his mom and Lally and Jools all sitting around the kitchen table with the tarot cards out, taking a long time wasn't a bad thing.

It felt good to walk along and think. Think about Cilla and how happy he was with her, and how sweet she was, and how patient she was with him, and how pretty she was, and how good she was at photography, and how smart she was, and how great she was generally.

It also felt good to walk along and not-think. Not-think, specifically, about Destiny. Not-think about how sexy she was, and that cute way she had of talking, and the funny things she said. He was so relieved to be not-thinking about all those things. To not-think about how nice it was to kiss her. How soft her hair was, how pretty it looked falling down her back, how the tips of it curled up just so. All week, he'd found Destiny bubbling to the surface of his thoughts, and it was good to walk down to the supermarket and not give her a moment's thought.

Of course, it didn't help any that Frank McCartney was his English teacher.

All week he'd kept looking at Mr. McCartney, wondering if Destiny had mentioned him to her brother—the mere thought of their conversation brought out a cold sweat. And Beatle couldn't be sure, but it seemed to him that a couple of times McCartney had looked at him strangely, as if he knew something Beatle didn't. He could imagine how a conversation between Destiny and her brother might have panned out:

"Met a student of yours," she might have said.

"Yeah? Who?"

"Guy called Beatle."

"Oh yeah. Beatle. Goes out with one of my other students, Cilla."

"Oh."

Or this:

"Hooked up with a student of yours over the weekend. Guy called Beatle."

"But Beatle's got a girlfriend."

"He can't."

"He does."

Or maybe it would have gone this way: "What do you mean you hooked up with Beatle? He's got a girlfriend. The slimy sleazebag. I'll tell you what I'm going to do. I'm going to haul him up in front of assembly this week and tell the whole school that he two-timed his girlfriend. And I'm going to fail him on every one of his exams. And I'm going to speak to the head examiners—who all happen to be friends of mine—and give them his student number so that he fails his end-of-year exams as well."

It had the potential for disaster. As soon as she'd mentioned that Mr. McCartney was her brother that first night, he should have stepped back and let the opportunity pass him by. But when opportunity has these insanely big red lips and this long dark hair and a cute way of talking and a sparkle in its eye, it's difficult to say "*Sayonara*" and keep on trucking.

He turned down the lane that ran beside the train line and admired the gigantic faces someone had graffitied onto the factory wall; they must have been ten feet tall, each face, and about twelve feet off the ground. How the artists had managed it, he couldn't even hazard a guess.

The thing was, the stupid thing was, even if he kissed her the first night, he definitely should have given her a wide berth the next day. What had gotten into him? Asking her on a picnic, for god's sake. That had taken it from being this one-night-stand thing that could be passed off as a drunken fling to a sober-and-actively-pursuing daytime activity, which had much more serious consequences if Cilla ever found out.

But Beatle needed to keep things in perspective. It was highly unlikely that Mr. McCartney was going to announce to the school that Beatle had hooked up with Destiny over the weekend. Mr. McCartney might find out about it, he might think Beatle was an asshole, and he might even give him a bad grade, but he was hardly going to sit down and start gossiping with the students about it. There wasn't a chance in hell Cilla would find out through Mr. McCartney. Right?

Beatle just had to keep his head. Not blow it by acting too guilty.

Beatle got to the supermarket, bought cigarettes, three loaves of bread, and three cartons of milk. Went back down the lane, past the graffiti faces, and kicked a bottle off the path. Crossed over Gold Street and turned down Grosvenor, walking along the footpath, squeezing past the garbage bins in front of the blocks of apartments. And that's when he saw them: the couple in the car.

Maybe it was the school uniform that got his attention.

Maybe there really is a telepathic thing that goes on between twins that compelled him to look.

Maybe it was *destiny*.

Whatever the reason, as Beatle walked down Grosvenor Street, he noticed the motorcycle first—in very good condition, it was—and then he noticed the old Ford Fairlane, 1960s model, blue, parked by the side of the road. In the front seat, a guy and a girl were going for it. Not having sex, but kissing like they might as well be. The girl had blonde hair, a bit messy, pulled back in a ponytail. And she was wearing a school uniform. Green, with red trim. The uniform from Beatle's school. Which made Beatle look a bit closer and realize it was Winsome.

His sister was sitting in the front seat of a car half-way down Grosvenor Street, kissing some guy. Some guy

Beatle didn't recognize. Although as he walked past them, the guy started to look more familiar. And that's when Beatle saw exactly who it was that Winsome was kissing.

It was Frank McCartney.

Their English teacher.

Destiny's brother.

Beatle had gotten home and dumped the three loaves, milk, and cigarettes on the kitchen table to a smoky "thanks" from his mom, Lally, and Jools, then gone straight to his bedroom, sat on his bed, and tried to unscramble his thoughts.

Morally, he didn't have a problem.

If his sister wanted to hook up with their English teacher, then more power to her.

She was eighteen. Whatever rocked her world.

But in this particular circumstance, he couldn't afford to be all "live and let live" about it. Since Winsome had hooked up with Mr. McCartney, the chances of her finding out about Destiny weren't just high, they were almost a dead certainty. And if Winsome found out about Destiny, it was only a matter of moments before she'd be telling Cilla.

He had only one option: he had to convince Winsome to stop snogging Mr. McCartney. It was as simple as that.

Beatle sat at his desk, trying to get a grasp on how, exactly, he should handle it. The Winsome-snogging-McCartney situation.

He could tell his mom what he'd seen and get her to speak to Winsome about it. But Beatle knew there wasn't a hope in hell that Winsome would actually listen to a thing their mom had to say.

Winsome hadn't paid attention to their mom's opinion for a long time, which is probably why their mom had resorted over the past few years to what Beatle thought of as "newspaper conversations."

It was a clear enough strategy: their mom would find an article in a newspaper or magazine, cut it out, then when Winsome got home, their mom would say, "Thought you might be interested in this" and push the article across the table to Winsome. Winsome would then glance down at it, see that it was about something that was of little or no interest to her at all—for example, whether teenage girls should be having sex—raise her eyes, and tell their mom she'd read it later. Then leave it on the table until their mom reluctantly threw it in the recycle bin a few days later. Unread and unloved.

But despite the fact that Winsome and their mom only had "newspaper conversations" these days, and despite the fact that the "newspaper conversations" didn't seem to have a great strike rate, Beatle still thought it might be worth getting their mom to discuss it rather than him.

He picked up the dice on his desk and rattled them in his hand, feeling the plastic warm up with his body heat.

Odds, he'd get his mom to have a word with Winsome. Evens, he'd have to do it.

He threw the dice. They balanced on their corners for a moment, then tipped over to display two black dots, one on each. Snake eyes.

Evens.

Beatle blew on the dice as he tried to decide what his next angle should be. How to convince Winsome to dump McCartney. What he could say that would get her to stop hooking up with him. And then he got struck with a lightning bolt of inspiration.

Cilla.

If anyone could convince Winsome to do something, it was Cilla. They weren't best friends for nothing.

He swilled the dice in the cup of his hand, opened his palm, and released the dice slowly, like a caress, onto his desk.

Odds, he'd get Cilla to talk to Winsome.

Evens, it was still his gig.

A four and a two. Six. Evens.

Shit.

Best out of three.

He rolled the dice again. Eight. Shit. And one last time for luck. . . . Six again.

Shit.

So he put the dice down and called Toby instead.

"What are you doing?" Beatle asked.

"Nothing. What about you?"

"Nada. You wanna go shoot some pool?"

There was a pause.

"Haven't you got a math exam tomorrow?" Toby asked.

"Yeah."

"Oh. Well, yeah, sure. Pool sounds good. What time?"

"Now."

Toby paused again. And then he said, "Sure. See ya there."

The Espy Hotel is on the Esplanade in St Kilda, right across the road from the beach. A grand old white building with flaky paint reminiscent of someone's badly sun-burnt back, with great swathes of skin ready to be peeled off. There's no question that about a hundred years ago it would have been one of Melbourne's most elegant hotels; however, it is now one of the grungiest pubs. Sticky carpet, graffiti on the booths, massive bouncers standing in the entrance like those statues with the ugly faces to scare away evil spirits—only these guys have ugly faces to scare away the evil people once they've had too many spirits. Many many years worth of cigarette smoke have added a caramelized veneer to the walls and ceiling. All of these things account for the Espy's extreme popularity.

The pool tables are out the back.

Toby racked up the balls on one of the tables, then chalked his cue and belted the bejesus out of the white ball, successfully sinking the eleven.

"I've got big balls," Toby said as he started stalking the

circumference of the pool table, trying to gauge the best angle and the best ball to go for.

"Not what I've heard," Beatle said. A standard response. Toby grinned but didn't take his eyes off the table. The hunter, assessing his prey.

The number twelve was right over the pocket, except one of Beatle's balls was directly between it and the white ball. Toby watched the twelve for a moment, calculating inside his head whether he could ricochet off the cushion and get the ball in, but decided against it and started stalking the table again, leaving the number twelve for when it could be picked off more easily. The number ten was a better bet, so he angled his cue at the white ball and aiming for the ten, pulled back his arm like the spring of a pinball machine, then jabbed neatly at the white ball, sending it rocketing across the table.

"Shit," said Toby as the ten bounced against the cushion and rolled to an awkward position at the side of the pocket.

"Close," said Beatle, "but no cigar."

Beatle leaned over the table and smashed the number two ball into the top left-hand pocket, then went for the number four. Bam, in it went. Toby didn't say a thing. Beatle kept his chin close to the green felt as he lined up the number three, but didn't quite get the angle he was after and the number three ball went scooting lamely across the table, finally coming to rest in no-man's-land.

"Close, but no cigar," Toby echoed. "Actually, not really that close even."

Beatle didn't respond, just stepped back from the table to watch Toby go for gold.

Toby adjusted his legs and leaned back over the table. He splayed his fingers on the felt and tested the pool cue gently between his thumb and second finger.

Beatle leaned against the wall and watched Toby give the white ball a shove with his cue, sending the nine ball into a side pocket. Beatle rested the end of his cue on the ground, his chin settling onto the tip and said, as casually as he could manage, "I was wanting your help with something."

"Yeah?" Toby said, not looking up. "Your game?"

"Piss off. No, Winsome."

"I hardly think I'd be able to help with her."

Winsome had a reputation among Beatle and his friends for being prickly. But only because she was. She was particularly prickly with Beatle, but her barbs had been known to stick into Toby and Magnus as well, if they went too close.

Beatle didn't remember quite what the turning point had been, the moment that made the difference between him and Winsome getting along as twins are expected to . . . and then not.

They used to be built-in friends for each other, no matter what boring party their dad dragged them along for, or what boring barbecue their mom hauled them off to. And then one day, Winsome didn't want to play anymore, barely wanted to talk to him even.

He remembered everyone always telling them how lucky they were to be twins. Asking what it was like. Treating them like mini-celebrities.

As soon as an adult heard they were twins, they'd coo and cluck and just about tickle them under their chins, the idea of twins being inherently adorable. And then whoever it was would look at them more closely, as if trying to see the inexplicable "twin thing" that must go on between them. The connection. The bond. The magic of being a twin.

"What's it like being a twin?" someone would ask, and Beatle would shrug and say, "Dunno. What's it like *not* being a twin?" which he thought was a very clever way of answering the question.

If he ever gave it much thought, he figured it was probably the same as being brother and sister, except maybe a bit different because they were the same age. Except on the eighteenth of December, when Beatle turned a new age, and Winsome stayed the same until her birthday on the first of February.

"You were in the womb together," their mom would

say. "Of course it's different from a normal brother and sister. It has to affect you. It can't possibly not. From the moment you were conceived," and Winsome would screw up her face at the word "conceive" because everyone knows what "conceive" really means, and no one wants to think about their folks doing it, "you've been together. Jostling for position, bumping into each other. You know that twins have been documented playing in the womb together, don't you? Even though you might not have been consciously aware of each other, subconsciously you knew you had someone with you at all times. There's a connection that can't be denied."

By this time, Beatle and Winsome had usually left the room.

But their mom would usually follow them into the kitchen, or wherever they'd gone, to continue her sermon.

"So that's why I don't understand the two of you not getting along now," she'd say. "All your lives you've been together. Slept in the same womb. Same room. Same crib. Just because you're teenagers doesn't mean you suddenly have to hate each other."

This was usually following some fight or other over the remote control or the computer or Beatle slurping too loudly as he ate his after-school bowl of Cheerios.

"We don't hate each other," Beatle would point out,

slurping his cereal for extra emphasis. "'Hate' is too strong a word. 'Detest' maybe."

"Abhor?" Winsome would suggest.

Beatle would think a moment.

"'Abhor' is a little pretentious," he'd say, "but the feeling is right. How about 'revolted by'?"

"Perfect," Winsome would say, nodding. "I'm revolted by him," she'd announce, turning back to their mom.

"And I'm revolted by her," Beatle would say, grinning at their mom. "So you should be happy we agree on something."

And their mom would click her tongue and leave the room.

Beatle rested his hip against the table and watched Toby sink another ball.

"She's hooked up with McCartney."

"McCartney who?"

"From school. You know. English."

Toby looked up and raised his eyebrows.

"Whoa."

"Yeah. And I need to convince her to give it up."

Toby stood and stared at Beatle, the game momentarily forgotten.

"One: good luck with that. Two: why would you bother? McCartney's not much older than us; he's probably the same age as Matt." Matt being Winsome's last boyfriend. "He seems like a good guy. And I hardly think he'd be taking advantage of her—she's too smart for that. I wouldn't worry about it."

Of course he wouldn't worry about it. That was because he didn't know how much there actually was to worry about.

Beatle chewed his lip, not sure how much to tell. The fact that McCartney had a sister named Destiny. The fact that Beatle had hooked up with Destiny. The fact that Beatle was scared as shit that if Winsome and McCartney were together, the chances of Cilla hearing about Beatle's little . . . flirtation . . . were a dead certainty.

Beatle looked at Toby. WTF, he'd have to tell it all.

A few days later Destiny got the first phone call.

The one that started with heavy breathing and ended with her hanging up the phone, figuring it was a wrong number or some random creep making random calls.

She just listened for a moment to the heavy breathing, said "hello" a couple of times to give the person a chance to reply—who knew, it might be someone whose cell phone was out of range, and the heavy breathing wasn't heavy breathing at all but something far less sinister—then shrugged and hung up the phone.

Nothing to report so far.

Move along, people, nothing to see here.

Later that same night, the phone rang again a couple of times, and when she picked it up she heard that same heavy breathing on the other end.

And hung up.

The next time the phone rang, Destiny left it for some-one else to answer. Her mom picked it up, then hung up right away with a click of her tongue and a shake of her head.

Next time the phone rang, Faith answered it and got no response, no breathing.

Ern was next to pick up the no-phone. This time the caller hung up before they could be hung up on.

It struck Destiny as strange, but nothing to worry about.

*B*eatle got home from the Espy and found Winsome on the couch, watching TV. He settled down on the couch next to her.

"What're you doing?" he asked.

"What do you think?" she said. "No, I'm not going to tell you. You've got to guess."

"Watching TV."

"Correct. That was fun. And now, I'd better get back to it."

She continued watching the screen, the light flickering over her face.

"Evil," Beatle said, using a nickname they hadn't used for each other in ages. It was one of those typical twin questions that they got asked every so often—which one's the evil twin? And they'd each say the other was, and when they were ten and eleven and twelve, they'd even called each other Evil for a while there, as a bit of a joke. But since they'd hit about fourteen, they hadn't used it. It had been Win and Beat, if they bothered speaking at all.

But tonight he needed her to listen to him. He needed to convince her.

"Number one," Toby had said as he slam-dunked the black ball into the side-corner pocket, "you need to sweet talk her"—which Beatle doubted was even possible. But calling her "Evil" was Beatle's version of sweet talk. Reminding her of the fun they used to have when they were kids.

"So, Evil," he said, "I saw you with McCartney tonight."

Winsome didn't answer, but he could tell by the way she bit her lip that she was listening.

"I just think you need to be careful," he continued. "I mean, he's our English teacher. I think it's really stupid to be hooking up with him when he's grading your exams and stuff."

Winsome scratched at her neck.

Beatle barged forward.

"Number two," Toby had said as he racked up the triangle of balls for another game, "make it seem like the sensible thing to do. Appeal to her better nature."

"I mean, it's only early in the year," Beatle said to Winsome, "and if things don't work out with him, he might get vindictive and lower your grade or something. And if you get caught by another teacher, you'll probably get expelled. And he'll get fired. I think you're insane to even try it."

Winsome looked over at him.

"Where did you see us?" she asked softly.

"On Grosvenor Street. In his car."

"Oh."

They both sat there, thinking their own thoughts. His thoughts mainly consisted of "Stop seeing him. Don't find out about Destiny. Stop seeing him. Don't find out about Destiny," and her thoughts consisted of who knew what?

"How long's it been going on for?" Beatle finally asked, after Winsome said exactly nothing.

Winsome pushed her hair off her face.

"Couple of months."

"Couple of months?" Beatle said, his eyebrows shooting up. Shows how much he knew.

"The Falls Festival. Remember we saw him there?"

"Yeah."

"Well," and she licked her lips, as if testing the platform that she was about to launch her confession from. She scratched her nose, then wiped her hand across her face. "I hooked up with him there, and I've been kind of seeing him ever since." She coughed uncomfortably, then went on. "I mean, I know dating your English teacher isn't generally done, but he wasn't our English teacher then. He was just one of the random teachers from school who happened to be very cute. It wasn't until I rocked up to school at the start of this year that I found out I was going to be in his class. He didn't know, either. I was supposed to be with Mr. Edgar, but then they had to switch things around for whatever reason and now I'm in with Frank, but it's fine. Don't worry about it. No one's going to find out."

Beatle studied Winsome as she kept her eyes carefully focused on the TV, arms folded across her chest. She was definitely avoiding looking at him.

It was hard for Beatle to tell if Winsome was pretty or not. He was too close to her—knew her features too well—to be able to tell if hers was a face that reeled you in from first viewing or if it was only once you got to know her that you found her attractive. It seemed to him that she had a fairly plain face. A serviceable face. A symmetrical face. Nothing that was overly anything in particular. A mouth that curved up, and was maybe a fraction bigger than the rest of her face warranted. Eyebrows that were neat. Twenty-twenty eyes that were deep brown in color. A nose that was neither here nor there, not too big, but not particularly perky and cute. It was a nose that breathed, did its job, without being too in your face. Or too on her face.

But something about her face seemed to draw people in. Maybe it was the very ordinariness of it that people liked. It was so bland that you could grow things on it. Emotions, for example. Yours.

Why you'd want to was beyond Beatle, but other people seemed to adore her.

Beatle had watched her enough times to know her *modus operandi*, to have worked out what drew people to her. She'd lightly touch a person's arm and drop her voice so that they'd have to lean in to her and *snap*, they'd be caught. Like a fish dangling at the end of a line—but not struggling, not trying to get away, immersing themselves instead in the tangle of her personality. It was like she was a people-whisperer. She'd watch someone, look into their eyes, duck her head so that she could see inside them, get in under their eyelashes. When she first met a person, it was as if she wanted to find out everything about them. She'd ask questions that no one else would be game to ask. Digging digging digging, always trying to find out more. Scratching away at them until she got under their skin. People fascinated her so much, the very people who fascinated her became fascinated *by* her.

Everyone fell for her. Always. Boys at school. Boys at parties. Matt.

"Is that why you and Matt split up?" Beatle asked.

"No," she said, in a voice that momentarily rose, then dropped back down. "Definitely not. It was way after Matt that I got together with Frank."

Winsome pushed her hair behind her ear, bit her lip, then kept talking.

"You know," she said, "Matt was kind of serious about us. As in, kind of too serious. I just want to have a good time. That's what I have with Frank. A good time. He's good fun. With Matt, it was always 'us' this and 'we' that, and to be honest, it was a bit more heavy than I wanted."

Beatle knew that feeling. The feeling of being hemmed in. Stuck. The word "rut" seemed strangely appropriate.

"But what are you going to do?" Beatle asked. "You can't keep seeing him. He's a teacher. He's *your* teacher."

Winsome shrugged, eyes firmly on the TV screen.

"Well, I'll be finished with school at the end of the year," she said. "We just have to keep it quiet until then."

Sure. Keeping things secret was exactly what Beatle was after, but he doubted he could keep his secret if Winsome kept her secret.

"Does anyone else know?" Beatle asked.

"Cilla."

"Cilla?"

"Yeah. But I made her promise not to tell anyone."

Beatle felt like a balloon was deflating inside his stomach.

"You made her promise not to tell me?" he asked.

"Well, not you specifically, but yeah. I mean, it's not like it's any of your business, is it?"

Yeah, it was his business. It was definitely his business.

"She even came with me one day to check out his house," Winsome continued, leaning back against the couch and grinning to herself. "He lives in this huge joint in Kew. With his folks. They must be loaded. You should see the place."

"You've met his family?" Beatle asked, panic rising like bile.

"No. Of course not. They'd freak if they knew he was seeing one of his students. Apparently they're very 'respectable' and everything has to be just so. Cilla and I only went and had a look."

"Just you and Cilla?"

"Yeah. Just to see. I mean, I didn't tell him. I wouldn't want him to think I was a stalker or anything. We were bored. It was something to do."

Beatle didn't know what to say. All the arguments Toby had given him: "it's immoral," "he could lose his job," "you might get expelled," all seemed wet and pathetic and not even slightly likely to persuade her.

And that was a problem.

"Has he mentioned me?" Beatle asked, watching her carefully to see her expression.

"What?" Winsome said, looking at him as if he were mad. "What would he say about you? 'Gee, your brother's cool'? 'Handsome'? 'I'd really like to get to know him'?

Something along those lines?"

"I don't know. I just wondered if you'd spoken about me."

"No. We discuss other things than my brother and my family. Oddly enough."

"Do you ever talk about his family?"

Winsome stared at him.

"What is this? Twenty questions? Yeah, sometimes we talk about his family. Occasionally we talk about mine. Usually though, we have better things to talk about. And now, if you don't mind," she said, turning her attention back to the television, "it's been real fun catching up with you; we must do it again sometime. . . . " And then she did this flicking motion with her fingers. International sign language for "piss off."

This wasn't going at all the way he'd planned. He'd known it wasn't going to be easy, but he'd assumed there was going to be some margin for persuasion.

Beatle went to his bedroom. It seemed to him there were three options:

1) Hope Destiny didn't mention his name to Frank.

2) Deny deny deny if Winsome ever found out.

3) Confess all.

He wasn't happy with Option 1.

He wasn't happy with Option 2.

And Option 3 clearly wasn't an option at all.

What Beatle really needed was a fourth option.

Something that nailed the problem of Winsome and Frank McCartney.

Option Number 4.

He'd have to come up with something.

$\mathcal{D}$estiny sat at the kitchen table, wet hair up in a towel, glasses on, glum chin in glum hand—watching Hope do the cryptic crossword.

"This one's easy, I'm sure," Hope said, tapping at seventeen-across with her pencil. "*After gold? Then the leader in charge is genuine! Nine letters.*"

She started scribbling in the margin of the newspaper, muttering to herself as she went.

"Gold is 'au,'" she said, writing down the chemical symbol for gold. "And *in charge* is 'i-c,'" she said, writing "ic" down in the margin of the paper. "So it's 'au' something something with 'ic' in there somewhere."

Destiny looked down at the puzzle on the table, then nibbled at her fingernail. She watched as Hope pushed her blonde hair back behind her ear, then stuck the end of the pencil in her mouth, as if it would help her think.

Of all Destiny's sisters, Hope was the most opposite of her. Where Destiny was dark, Hope was pale, where Destiny's hair curled, Hope's hung straight as a sheet, where Destiny would laugh, Hope stayed somber.

"Come on," Hope said through the pencil, "I'm sure this is an easy one."

It was a bit of a tradition between the two of them. Each day they'd claim the cryptic as theirs to solve. The Sudoku was the province of Ern and their mom, the nine-letter word was always done by Frank, but the cryptic was Hope and Destiny's domain.

Destiny couldn't think of a single word. The clues weren't prompting any thoughts inside her head. She was a font of nothingness.

This whole waiting thing was horrible, and Destiny could understand why a lot of girls took the initiative and ended up calling the boys themselves. You call a boy, the whole waiting-by-the-phone thing is gone with the touch of a finger. But Destiny had a mother who was dead-against calling boys.

"If a boy's interested," her mom maintained, "he'll call. If he's not interested, he won't call. So if he's not interested, what's the point in calling him yourself?"

Destiny's dad would usually weigh in at about this time.

"It's true," he'd say, nodding wisely and propping his glasses on the end of his nose to add a seriousness to his words. "Men are hunters, women are gatherers. It's that whole primitive thing. It's hardwired into us. Men like the hunt. They like the chase. If a woman calls them, the chase is over. The fun has gone out of it. You've shown your trump card—that you're interested—so the hunt is finished. You've got to keep them on their toes for as long as you can."

Not that Destiny necessarily agreed with half the garbage that spouted out of their mouths, but on the subject of calling boys, she was in a no-go zone. She'd never called a boy in her life (unless they'd been together for a while), and she doubted she ever would.

So, even though she was itching to speak to him, calling Beatle wasn't an option.

"Have you heard from that guy?" Hope asked, as if reading her thoughts.

It was eerie the way Hope did that sometimes. It was like she was finely attuned to any feelings of helplessness or depression and would swoop in like a seagull who's spotted a crumb of misery.

"No," Destiny said, not even bothering to lift her chin from her hand as she shook her head. "It's a week since I last saw him. I can't believe he didn't call. We had such a good time together. I don't get it."

He could have at least paid her the common courtesy of making it extremely obvious that he was using her. But everything he'd done, the way he'd acted, the way he'd looked at her had seemed so . . .

"Ooh, *authentic*," Destiny said suddenly, grabbing

the pencil from Hope and scribbling the letters into the squares of seventeen-across.

After gold? Then the leader in charge is genuine!

"The leader of the word 'the' is 't,'" Destiny explained to Hope, showing how smart she was, "and you've already got 'au' and 'ic,' and I suppose 'then' just goes in because it fits. "*Is genuine.* Authentic."

The thing with cryptics, the trick, is there are common threads in the clues, and once you've done a few of them, you notice triggers—certain clues that mean certain letters. For example, "The Queen" means "er," because the Queen is Elizabeth Regina, so ER are her initials. Other clues might mean that a particular word is an anagram, or that it's written backwards. Once you've done them for a while, you pick up the triggers. The tricks of the trade. So you can often construct a word simply by hobbling together the clues.

"That's good," said Hope, nodding to herself. "Well done. Very clever."

"Why, thank you," said Destiny, nodding her head as if she were curtseying, her towel turban tipping woozily.

"Not you," said Hope with a slow eye-roll. "The puzzle. Quite a clever clue."

"And clever me for figuring it out."

Destiny unwrapped the towel from around her hair and pushed the messy mop-top off her face.

"Oh, I don't know about that," said Hope. "We already had half of it. A lucky guess, I'd say."

Destiny slung the towel over her shoulder and punched Hope in the arm.

"How's that for a lucky guess? I thought I might punch you in the arm, and then I actually did."

Hope looked up at Destiny, then looked back down at the newspaper. She wasn't even going to dignify Destiny's punch with an answer.

And then Faith came into the kitchen and went over to the laundry room, where their mom was doing whatever it is mothers do inside laundry rooms.

"Can you not touch my underwear?" Faith said. "You know I don't like anyone touching it."

Their mom came to the doorway and put her hands on her hips.

"I haven't touched your underwear," she said. "It's more than my life's worth to touch any of your things."

Yes, Faith was quite picky about her lingerie. She handwashed it each night, hung it out to dry on a separate part of the clothesline in the yard, and didn't like it being plonked in the laundry basket with all the other pedestrian items of clothing that everyone else in the family wore.

She even went so far as to have a theory on underwear.

"You know how each morning you look in your wardrobe and decide what to wear?" she had told them. "Or, you guys look in MY wardrobe and decide what to wear. Well, before I decide what I'm going to wear, I decide what I'm going to wear UNDERNEATH what I'm going to wear. You know what I mean? Because the lingerie I choose has this, like, profound impact on my mood for the day."

"Really?" Hope had replied, shaking her head as if she couldn't quite believe she was related to someone as frivolous as Faith.

"Yeah. Absolutely. Like, if I'm in a good mood, I'll put on my, you know, my bright blue bra and underwear with all the different colored dots all over them? And then all day I feel really up and happy. Or, if I'm feeling a bit quieter and more serious, or say if I think it's going to be a tough day at work and really busy, I'll put on my set with the army camouflage pattern and the khaki lace. And then I've got my Roma set," "Roma" with a rolled R to make it more Italian sounding, "for if I've got something really special happening and I want things to go well."

That, for sure, was a beautiful set of lingerie. Faith had brought it home from her trip backpacking around Europe last summer. She didn't bring anything else home—no souvenirs, no presents for the family—but she brought these showy little peacocky bits of silky nothingness, which had set her back a small fortune. Steely blue silk with exotic flowers and delicate dragonflies intricately hand-embroidered over each slither of fabric, and the bra had the thinnest, shoe-string-strappiest straps you've ever seen, and the underwear had the same thin thin thin straps linking the front flimsy piece of cloth with the back flimsy piece of froth.

"It's my Roma," with a rolled R, "set that's gone," Faith said, shaking her head. "I hung it out last night and now it's not there."

"Well," said their mom, "it must be somewhere. Maybe you took it up to your room and forgot you'd already taken it off the line. It has to be somewhere. No one's taken it."

No one's. Taken. It.

*C*illa had told Beatle the news that morning in Photography.

The news about her dad going certifiably mad.

"He cracked this morning," she said, spreading out all the photos she'd processed over the past few weeks and putting red dots on the ones she thought might make up part of her project, "about how little studying I'm doing, and how important this year is, and how he thinks I'm spending too much time with you, and over at your place, so he's got this new regime," and when she said "regime" she put finger quotes around the word, "where I have to do at least three hours of studying a night, and I'm not allowed to go out except to official events. It's like he's gone certifiably mad or something. And I said to him, it's my life, I can do what I like. I'm eighteen years old. If I only want to study a bit, then that's fine, and my grades are good enough at the moment, but he said good enough isn't good enough, that he wants me to do brilliantly, that I'm capable of brilliant, not good enough, and I told him he was forcing me to commit social suicide, I mean, seriously, so he said I could go out one night a week with friends, but had to be home by eleven," and here she laughed a bitter little laugh, "and I said gee, thanks, you're too kind," sarcasm heavy. "So basically, I'm not allowed out except one night a week, and only late if I've got an official party to go to."

"But what about just coming around to my place to chill?" Beatle asked.

"Banned."

"What about after school?"

"For a limited time only," she said, sounding like an ad.

"What about during the day on the weekend?"

"Only if I've finished my three hours a day of homework."

"But I don't get it. Why aren't you allowed out at night? If you've done your homework, what difference does it make?" Beatle asked, putting a red dot on one of his favorite photos that Cilla hadn't marked.

"Dad said if I go out, I'm too tired the next day to do much studying. Which is a joke, because I do homework whether I'm hungover or not. But he said if I go out and drink, my brain's not as switched on as if I've had an early night. There's nothing I can do to convince him. And when I spoke to Mum about it, she said that Dad doesn't put many demands on me, so if that's what he wants, that's how it's gotta be. It's like she's so weak, she won't even stand up to him for me."

"So you can't even come 'round tonight and watch TV?" Beatle checked. "Just for a couple of hours?"

"Nuh. Nada. Not if we're going out tomorrow night with Amelia and Nique and Toby and those guys."

"Oh," Beatle had said. "Well . . . bummer."

And he'd really meant it. It was a bummer that her dad was cracking down on her and coming up with "regimes" that were going to limit her social life. That he wasn't going to be able to see her as often.

So you can imagine his surprise when, after Photography, he found his very own fingers secretly scrolling through his address book until Destiny's number came up on the screen. And then—the impertinence of his very own body—his thumb pressed the "dial" button.

And his arm put the phone up to his very own ear and waited while the number rang.

It was only a matter of time before she was going to damn well answer.

The question was: What was his mouth going to do about it?

$\mathcal{D}$estiny sat on the desk in the art room, scribbling ideas down in her sketchpad for her next piece.

"You shouldn't be up there," Mathilde said, looking at Destiny from the computer where she had a shot of a stalk of wheat on the screen. "You know what Miss Miller says about sitting on desks."

"You won't get married," Netta said.

"According to Miss Miller," Destiny added. "And I hardly think Miss Miller would know about getting married."

"Exactly," said Mathilde. "Miss Miller wouldn't have a clue about getting married, and maybe the fact is, she sat on a desk when she was younger and that's why she's single today."

"Ooh." Destiny waggled her fingers at Mathilde to show how "spooky" that link was. "Maybe you're right."

"No question she's right," said Netta, looking at the gigantic face she was sketching onto a canvas. "If anyone knows about being a spinster, it's Miss Miller. You should take her warnings seriously, young lady."

Netta tapped her finger in Destiny's general direction.

Netta's project was going to consist of a series of extreme close-ups of faces on enormous canvases, faces that were about seven times larger than the real thing, and the extraordinary detail she was going into was quite mesmerizing to watch.

She had the woman from the fruit shop down on Glenferrie Road; the man from the key-cutting place; her neighbor, Mr. Castigan, whose wife had died last year; Mathilde, chin in hand; and her grandma with her exquisitely lined face.

"Yeah, well, Miss Miller's probably right; what with Beatle's lack of interest and not-calling, I probably will be a spinster," Destiny said, wanting to mention Beatle's name a couple more times before shelving him in a dark and dusty corner of her head.

Mathilde and Netta thought a moment, then nodded.

"Probably," they both agreed.

Destiny threw an eraser at Netta, who was closer.

"Ow."

"Sorry. Slipped," Destiny said.

Netta looked up at her with her famous no-expression face—a mix of slackened eyes and slackened mouth—then went back to her mammoth sketch of Mr. Castigan.

"I went on Beatle's Facebook page last night," Destiny said. "You wanna see?"

Mathilde and Netta looked up at her. What did she think?

Destiny went over to where Mathilde was on the computer.

"Shove over," she said.

"Hang on," Mathilde said. "I just want to finish tracing around this."

Mathilde was continuing with the stalker theme for her project, only she'd changed it from photographing Netta and Destiny in front of Ange's place (after all, who knew who Ange was, or even whether she was a girl or not?) and instead was using computer-generated imagery to explore her theme. She had one canvas called "Stalked," which consisted of stalks of wheat repeated across the page, but when you stood back, they made up the image of a frightened girl's face. Her second canvas was called "Snowdropping," and in it she showed a variety of white underwear and bras intertwined to make up snowflake shapes . . .

"Did you know there's an official term for stealing underwear off a clothesline?" she'd said the other day. "Snowdropping."

"No way," said Netta.

"Way," replied Mathilde.

. . . and her third canvas had tiny cameras making up an image of an old-fashioned phone with the words "Watching you" written across it.

Mr. Castles said he was pretty pleased with her idea, but he wanted her to push it more.

"If he tells me one more time I need to 'push my ideas,'" Mathilde said, "I'm going to push all right. Him, into a closet, and throw away the key."

Mathilde finished tracing around the stalk of wheat, then moved over for Destiny to show them Beatle's Facebook page.

His photo at the top was the Playboy bunny icon.

"Nice," said Netta. "Tasteful."

"Classy," agreed Mathilde.

"I know," said Destiny. "This is good, because it shows why we were so wrong for each other, anyway. How can I possibly be with a guy who has the Playboy bunny as his Facebook photo?"

"Well, you can't," said Mathilde. "Simple as that."

"Absolutely no way," agreed Netta. "Show us his friends."

They went through the photos of Beatle's friends, guys called Toby and Magnus and another guy called Bollo, and a chick called Evil and another one called Cilla, and Amelia and Nique and Wilbur and photos of parties he'd been to and a short film he'd shot of his buddies skateboarding, and then under the short film, just randomly there on the page, he'd written, "Well, the name's Beatle and i lyk bacon & eggs & cheese (mmmmmmmmmmmmmmmmm 61 slices of American cheese) um well i go to Elwood High and i skateboard weekends and yeah lyk so whatever." He had his age listed as ninety-four and a half.

"You don't think he's too old for you, do you?" asked Mathilde.

"That's why he hasn't called you," said Netta. "He's worried about the age difference."

"You're right," agreed Destiny. "It was never going to work. In fact," she added, clicking off his page, "I'm glad he didn't call. I'd go so far as to say him not-calling is one of the best things that's ever happened to me in my entire life."

"*One* of the best?" said Mathilde. "*The* best, I'd say."

"In fact," Destiny added, to make sure everyone knew she was serious this time, "even if he called now, no matter what, I wouldn't go out with him. He's a slacker about calling, has terrible taste in food, and he's old enough to be my grandpa."

"Great-grandpa," said Netta.

"I don't know what you saw in him, to be honest," said Mathilde.

"I never thought it was going to work," added Netta.

And at that moment, Destiny's phone rang.

"Hello?" she said.

There was no answer.

And then she heard, "Hi. Destiny?"

"Yeah."

"It's Beatle."

"Oh. Hi," she said, widening her eyes at Mathilde and Netta to let them know it was *him* on the phone. "How are you?"

"Yeah. Good. How have you been?" he asked.

"Not bad."

"Haven't spoken for a while," he said.

"No."

"I thought it might be good to catch up."

"Oh. Yeah. That'd be great," she said.

Who cared if it was day thirteen? Who cared if he'd just found the phone number in his jeans' pocket and decided to give her a call accidentally? Who cared if he was ninety-four and a half? Who cared if he overindulged in cheese? He was cute and he'd called and therefore, that was a good thing.

"You got anything on tonight? You wanna go see a movie or something?" he asked.

Destiny smiled.

"Yeah, for sure," she said.

"And I don't think it matters that it's thirteen days

since I last saw him," Destiny told Netta and Mathilde as soon as she got off the phone.

And Mathilde said, "Of course it doesn't. God, as if I'm one to talk. Josh never calls, but if I see him at a party I'll kiss him, anyway."

"It's all very well to have these rules and regulations," agreed Netta, sketching carefully at the lined mouth of Mr. Castigan, "but you certainly wouldn't want to live your life by them. In fact, maybe the main purpose of rules, the real reason they're created, is so you know when you've broken one."

And the three girls grinned: breaking rules being one of their favorite pastimes.

Beatle's resolve was firm when he got to Chadstone shopping mall that night.

He wasn't going to kiss her.

They were just going to have a friendly night. She was a nice girl. He liked her personality. Her lips held no sway over him. They'd go see a movie, have a chat, he'd check that she hadn't mentioned him to her brother, and then he'd go home.

Lips intact.

No problem.

Nothing shady or bad-boyfriend-y about it.

Just two friends catching up. In fact, it was so innocent

that he'd be quite happy to tell Cilla. He would. Except if he told Cilla, she'd ask him all these questions about "Who's Destiny?" and "Where did you meet her?" and "I've never heard of her," so it was easier not to tell the truth and say he was staying home instead.

But only because it was easier. Not because he was doing anything sneaky.

There was definitely going to be no kissing or carrying on. Maybe a friendly "hello" peck, and that was all.

He was going to be like a Zen Buddhist master about it all.

Friendly but distant.

Detached.

And then he saw her.

She was wearing a tight T-shirt with the word "Lamb" written across it in gothic writing. Her army fatigues slung from hip to hip like a hammock he'd like to crawl into on a lazy summer afternoon. She had that mouth of hers on her face. He grinned as she plonked down on the bench beside him. He couldn't help himself. It was a wide grin that said "Come and get me" rather than "Let's keep this on a strictly business footing."

"To the slaughter, eh?" he said.

"What?" she asked, her eyes crinkling as she smiled at him.

His eyes wandered down to the word that was drawled

fetchingly across her boobs.

"Lamb," he explained, nodding at her. "To the slaughter."

She laughed.

"God. Sacrificial virgins one day, lambs to the slaughter the next. You've got an interesting conversation style, I'll give you that," she said.

And that wasn't all she gave him by the end of the night.

*A*dmittedly, things hadn't gone strictly as planned for Beatle. Take, for example, that whole determination-not-to-kiss-her business; that had come unstuck once her lips were planted firmly on his.

But making sure she didn't mention him to her brother? Have a listen to how perfectly that panned out:

"So anyway," Destiny had said, looking at Beatle with a tilt to her head, "you haven't said anything to Frank about meeting me, have you?"

Beatle didn't answer for a moment. The thing he badly needed to know, *she* was asking him. Finally he said, "No. Should I have?"

The apples of Destiny's cheeks ripened as she smiled.

"You know what?" she said, shrugging a shoulder. "I'd rather you didn't. Not at this stage, anyway. He'll just rag me about it, and probably make a big deal about it with you, say something in class, and it would just be embarrassing. If I can give him one less piece of ammunition, that'd be a good thing. Is that weird?"

Beatle grinned at her.

"No," he said. "I totally get what you mean."

Convincing Destiny not to tell her brother?

Done. And done.

Saturday night was not-so-good. There was something wrong. Something making him feel all tense and irritable. A trapped feeling. A suffocating in his throat feeling. A this-girl-isn't-Destiny feeling.

He couldn't get Destiny's lips out of his head. And wished he didn't have to get them off his face. And her eyes, dark and sleepy-looking. And her hair, black and long and slightly wavy. And even her nose—kind of large but striking; it suited her perfectly, anchoring her eyes and drawing her whole face together.

The thing was, she was gorgeous and made him laugh. Telling him about a tapestry she'd stolen from her neighbor's front yard; the party she'd been to where the pool table had collapsed; her sister's crazy theory about underwear. She was a funny chick.

Beatle knew he wasn't being fair. It wasn't Cilla's fault. She was still the same girl. He was the one who'd changed.

But unfortunately, because of Destiny, Cilla was pissing him off.

Beatle wondered how those old guys who had affairs behind the backs of their wives managed it. They must have some kind of technique or system they followed. Putting people into drawers inside their heads and only pulling them out when they were there in the flesh.

Something his dad was probably quite good at, considering all the affairs he'd apparently had behind his mom's back.

Something that Beatle didn't want to get good at.

Beatle went to the bar and bought Cilla a bowl of chips and a drink. Even though she hadn't asked for either. A tasty treat that proved he was actually a good guy and not some two-timing bastard. Even though he was. But he wasn't going to go too far this time. Not like a couple of weeks ago when he was Captain Overboard with all the presents he got her. This time, he was Captain Sensible. Something small and appetizing and not too suspicious.

As he sat at the table, watching his friends talk and not really listening, Beatle started to feel pissed off. The whole fact that he had to go and buy her chips and a drink to make amends for not being altogether happy in their relationship kind of sucked. What he should do was take this as an opportunity to talk with Cilla about whether they still wanted to be together. Have an open discussion. They were both eighteen; they could manage an adult conversation.

And maybe, if he was lucky, Cilla would be feeling the same way. Maybe she'd met someone else, even.

What he was really hoping for, if he were to be completely honest, was for Cilla to break up with him.

Because in the end, when you break up with someone, you'd much rather have them dump you. When you know you don't want to be with someone anymore, the worst part of breaking up is having to tell them it's over. Because the whole thing about being with someone in the first place is that you like them. And if you've been with them for a while, you probably love them. Although, admittedly, you've probably skated past the love bit by the time you reach the wanting-to-break-up-with-them stage, but still, you like them. And to have to tell someone you like that it's over between you is a really hurtful thing to do. And if you can avoid hurting them, if you can somehow make it that they hurt you instead, you'd much rather do it that way.

Beatle looked across at Cilla and smiled at her.

Polite. Friendly.

What would be absolutely perfect would be for Cilla to say to him, "Beatle, we need to talk." And for her to then talk about how bored she was with him, and how she didn't find him attractive anymore, and how she thought maybe they'd simply been together too long, no hard feelings, and how maybe it was an accident that they'd gotten together in the first place, and how she'd felt sorry for him that day in the hospital, that's why she'd kissed him, not because she'd wanted to go out with him, and maybe she'd point out that she'd wanted to bust up with him for a while, but it was hard because Winsome was her best friend and she didn't want to damage that relationship, and then she'd admit that she'd started seeing someone else who she really liked, and Beatle would be upset, crushed actually, and everyone would feel sorry for him because Cilla had dumped him.

In the end, that was what he was really hoping for.

That—Beatle decided—would be the perfect way to finish things between them.

*T*he screen opens on two women, a pair of twins in their late thirties, with a little girl of about three sitting on one of their knees.

"My husband and I had been trying to get pregnant for ages," one of them says, her cheeks sucked in slightly as if she's chewed on them for too long and they're forever hollowed. "It had probably been a year, and nothing much seemed to be happening."

She breathes deeply and looks at the camera. Her mouth a grim, straight line. Her sister looks away from the camera, away from her twin.

"And then, Adele gets pregnant. Which was great, of course, and I was thrilled for her, but she wouldn't say who the father was, or how it had happened, or anything. Just kept saying it was a guy she'd had a one-night stand with and she didn't want to discuss it. Which, of course, is not like her. We tell each other everything. That's what twins do. But I figured it didn't matter who the dad was. She was having a baby, and because we're so close, it was like I was going to be having a baby, too. I mean, on the one hand it seemed kind of cruel—I'd been trying so hard for so long, and then she goes and gets pregnant from one night. I was happy for her, but unhappy for me at the same time. Do you know what I mean?"

Adele looks down at her daughter and pushes the little girl's hair behind her ear.

"The day Molly was born was beautiful but also painful for me." The sister puts her hand on the little girl's head, patting her. "Then, Dele started trying to get some money out of the father but was having trouble getting any support from him. She kept threatening legal proceedings, but he seemed to think she was bluffing. Then one morning I'm at home and there's a knock on the door. A process server, delivering a summons for my husband. To pay support for Adele's baby."

Adele begins chewing her lip.

Offscreen, a voice asks, "So your husband was the father of your sister's baby?"

"Exactly."

The twin who's talking pouts for a moment, looks down, then continues.

"I know a lot of people won't be able to understand this, and, I mean, at first I was devastated—ranting and raving and not talking to Adele—but in the end, you know, it's worked out well. Because I can't have children. Ever.

Endometriosis. I'm completely infertile. And my husband wouldn't have had a baby if it wasn't for my sister. So we all live together. And it works. It works for us. The alternative was for me to lose my husband or my sister, and I didn't, in the end, want to lose either. Rob and I were under tremendous pressure, and I think he just wanted to feel close to someone without worrying about whether they were going to get pregnant or not. And ironically, she did. One night, and she gets pregnant."

She stops talking for a moment, looks over at her sister, then resumes.

"It's funny; without the betrayal, we wouldn't have the happy ending. So is it worth it for this?" and she kisses the little toddler on the top of her head. "Of course. No question."

Offscreen, the interviewer asks a question. The twin laughs.

"Oh, sure. I'd still trust her with my life. I just wouldn't trust her with my husband."

Beatle called Destiny on Sunday afternoon.

"You know the number sixteen tram?" he said.

"The one that starts at far Kew," she said, throwing in the old joke, "through near Kew," she continued, "and down to St Kilda?"

"That's the one," Beatle said. "The one that goes past the Elwood Canal—the far canal . . ."

(Say it out loud, you should get it. Imagine an Australian accent, if that helps.)

Destiny laughed.

"That's good," she said. "I haven't heard that before."

". . . all the way to the near canal and down to St Kilda and into the city."

Destiny grinned.

"Yeah," she said. "I know it. What about it?"

"Well," Beatle went on, "say if I caught it from my joint down Balaclava Road in the direction of Kew . . ."

"Far Kew," Destiny added.

". . . far Kew, and say you caught it from your joint

down Glenferrie Road in the direction of St Kilda . . ."

"And the far canal."

"Exactly, and say we each got off somewhere in the middle, say, in Malvern somewhere, where would be a good place to meet? Hypothetically."

"Hypothetically when?"

"Hypothetically now."

"Well," Destiny said, taking a breath and thinking, "I don't know. How about—hypothetically, of course—Scream?"

Beatle smiled to himself. There it was underneath all her words, barely noticeable but then sometimes, with particular words, coming to the front. That slight lisp she had.

"Scream?" he said. "What is it?"

"It's this thing girls do when they're terrified."

Beatle grinned and didn't answer.

"It's also this ice-cream parlor," Destiny said, "just near the corner of Glenferrie and High Street. You know, as in *I scream, you scream, we all scream for ice cream*. It's pretty cool."

"Well, it would be cool, wouldn't it? Being an ice-cream parlor. Probably refrigerated even."

"Ha ha," Destiny said. "Anyway, so if, hypothetically, I was to put my French essay aside and come and meet you this afternoon, that's where I'd suggest."

"Imagine if we met there in half an hour," Beatle said.

"I can't even begin to imagine what that would be like," Destiny said.

Beatle hung up the phone.

And put his English essay to one side.

Scream is this kooky little ice-cream parlor with an old-fashioned sign hanging out front and booths inside that remind you of a sitcom and waitresses rollerblading up to take your order. An order that might sound something like, "We'll have one Strawberry Sundae Bloody Sunday and a Bountiful Beatific Banana Blitz," or "Two Kinky Kingpin Caramel Sundaes, thanks." Something along those lines.

Exactly the sort of thing Beatle wasn't supposed to have. Not if he stuck to his list of:

#1: Eat healthy and exercise regularly but not to extreme.

#2: Avoid fats, especially the ones in meat and butter. And probably the ones in donuts. And probably ice-cream sundaes.

#3: Monitor your blood pressure.

Et cetera and so on.

He grinned at Destiny, who was jammed into the booth beside him, her bare arm causing a crazy sensation in his stomach.

"So you're doing French, yeah?" Beatle asked as he ran his eye down the menu and thought about running his hands down her. "You good?"

She raised an eyebrow at him.

"*Très, très bien*," she said, the syllables growling in her throat like she were some kind of foreign film actress.

"Hmm. I can imagine you would be," Beatle said, leaning close to her. "You gonna go there once you finish school? Go travelling?"

Destiny shrugged.

"Yeah. Not for a while, though. I mean, I know everyone wants to do a year abroad and all that, but I'm wanting to get into graphic design, and if I do, I'm pretty pumped to go and start that. What about you?" she said, tipping her head towards him. "What do you want to do when you've finished?"

"Film school," he said. "College of the Arts."

"Right," she said, nodding. "That'd be brilliant. Is it hard to get into?"

Beatle tipped his head, too.

"Think so. You've got to have made a short film—I've already finished one, and I'm working on my next now, which is a kind of Melbourne version of *Romeo and Juliet*—and you've got to do this kind of test before they'll even give you an interview. You know, draw nine pictures to tell a story without using any words, give a synopsis for the film you'd like to make during your time at film school, that type of thing."

"Right," she said and smiled at him, then looked down at the menu. "So what are you going to have?"

Beatle checked out the list.

"Dunno," he said. "Maybe a Hunky-Dory Hokey-Pokey Crunch Sundae. How about you?"

"Oh, that's a shame," she said, "because that's what I'm having, and obviously you can't have what I'm having."

"Oh."

"No," she said. "Because otherwise we can't share. You'll have to have something else. Now, let me see," she said, running her finger down the list, and then tapping at one of the descriptions, "this was the other one I was thinking of having—a Mmmmmmmmmmint Sundae. You want that?"

Beatle grinned at her. "Well, it wasn't quite what I had in mind."

She clicked her tongue. "Hmm. Okay. Alternatively," she said, going back up the list, "you can have a Peeky Cheeky Pecadillo of Peach Sundae."

He leaned closer to her.

"That sounds good," he said.

"Or a Clever Classical Coffee Sundae," she noted,

looking up from the menu and tapping the description as if it were all decided. "They're your choices. Which one do you want?"

Beatle moved a smidgin closer.

"Can I have some thinking music while I decide?" he asked.

"Sure," she said and started humming a tuneless song; her mouth pushed out slightly as terrible noises—something like a dying animal would make—came out from between her perfect plump lips.

"God," he said. "That sounds awful. Here, let me help you with that." And he leaned forward and kissed her. "Anything to make that dreadful noise go away," he continued. "Desperate—times," he added, a kiss punctuating his words, "call—for desperate—measures."

*A*nd then there was Cilla. Outside school, first thing, Monday morning.

"Where were you last night?" she asked. "I called a couple of times, and Winsome said you hadn't been home all afternoon. What were you doing?"

Beatle had it all under control. Nothing to see here, people. Move along.

"I was location scouting for the film," he said.

"Oh. But I thought you had all the locations sorted," Cilla said, frowning at him.

Beatle looked away from her, over to where McCartney was crossing the school yard towards class. He wondered if his face had "Guilty" written all over it. Or "Out kissing another girl." "Spent afternoon with Destiny." Take your pick.

"Not all of them," he said, pushing his hair off his face. "I mean, I know pretty much where I want to shoot everything, but there were a couple of other places I wanted to have a look at."

"Oh." Cilla frowned some more. "What? By yourself?"

"Yeah."

Deepening furrows across her forehead.

"But why didn't you get Toby or Magnus to go with you?"

"Well, because it was a spur of the moment thing."

"Yeah?"

Clearly this wasn't a good enough answer.

"I wanted to go check out some other spots, and I didn't think to call anyone, to be honest."

To be dishonest.

"But I don't get it. Why didn't you get someone to go with you?"

"I don't always have to have a friend along," he said, an irritated snag in his voice. "I can do some things by myself, you know."

Cilla had better watch it with that frown or her face would stay that way.

"Oh. Well, what time did you get home?"

"I don't know, Cilla. Eight? Nine? I'm not sure. I wasn't checking my watch."

"Right."

Cilla pouted, her mouth now matching her forehead.

"And Winsome told you that I called?" she asked.

"Yeah."

"I called your cell."

"I had it turned off."

"Oh. So why didn't you call me back when you got home?"

Beatle sighed. What he wanted to say was, "Shut up. Just shut up and stop asking questions. I didn't call because I didn't want to. I didn't want to have a conversation with you—the one we're having now—because I wasn't in the mood. And I'm not in the mood for it now, but you keep crapping on about where were you, and why weren't you with anyone, and why didn't you call, and the fact is there are no answers I can give you that are going to satisfy you, so why don't we just go in to class and forget about it? Nothing I can say is going to be good enough for you, because it's all going to sound fake and wrong, because it *is* fake and wrong, and the only way you'll feel satisfied is if you know the truth, and there isn't a hope in hell I'm going to tell you the truth. So there's no point in having this conversation. End of story."

But instead he said, sounding slightly world weary, as if she were such a drag for being so demanding, "I was studying. I had tons to do. I've got to hand in that essay for English, and I wasn't even close to finishing it."

"So why did you go location scouting, if you hadn't finished your essay?"

"Oh, shit, Cilla, I don't know. Because I wanted to. Because I felt like it. Because I was being irresponsible and crazy and didn't do my homework until the last minute," he said.

Cilla stared at him.

"Right," she said, then turned and walked away, a hurt, wounded tilt to her body.

Beatle kicked at the ground.

If you know anything about superstitions, you'll know there is apparently a magical bond between a wound and the weapon that inflicted it. For example, if you're cut by a knife, you should get the knife and put it in a cold place to reduce any inflammation. If you've accidentally hurt someone and regret it, you should spit on the hand that gave the wound and the pain of the injured person will be alleviated immediately.

Beatle looked at Cilla walking up the school steps.

He didn't want to hurt her.

He regretted causing her pain.

He looked down at his hands and spat in the palm of each one.

But he doubted it would make any difference.

*T*hey say the Yarra River runs with its bottom close to the surface, all silt and scunge and mud running along the top. If you're a skateboarder in Melbourne—if you're really serious about it—you'll find yourself fairly regularly down at the skate bowl beside the Yarra River, hunkered down under the Swanston Street Bridge within stone-throwing distance of the glass towers that make up the city skyline. A free-balling yin to the stiff, uptight, corporate yang of stockbrokers and accountants and lawyers and whatever the hell else all those business-types do tucked up inside their fuck-off skyscrapers. With nothing but a big, upside-down river keeping the two worlds separate.

Beatle leaned against the rail of the stairs beside the skate bowl, his feet splayed to keep himself steady, the Yarra at his back, video camera at his eye—focused and rolling—as Toby tried to land a backside one-eighty down an eight set.

Toby ollied up, turned his body and board 180 degrees,

then started going down the stairs before tumbling over for the millionth time.

Magnus whooped and stuck his head up close into the lens of the camera.

"That was awesome," Magnus said, grinning, his mouth taking up the entire screen. Beatle lifted his head from the camera and looked at Toby.

"You're not using it," Toby said, leaning over to pick up his skateboard.

"We are for sure. It'll look wicked. Good for the opening credits maybe," Magnus suggested to Beatle, winding Toby up.

Toby turned back to the stairs. In the end, the only thing that mattered to him was landing this trick. He could punch the shit out of Magnus later.

They'd been at the skate bowl all afternoon. So far Toby had snapped two decks (scabbed seventy bucks off Beatle after snapping his first deck to buy the second one), snapped that, and now he was riding Magnus's board, ollying up, turning one-eighty, then tumbling down the steps, ollying up, turning one-eighty, tumbling down the steps, ollying up, fucking up, nearly getting it, losing his rhythm, confusing himself, morphing and changing it into another move, but never nailing the backside one-eighty that Beatle wanted to film him doing down the stairs.

"How about this for the opener?" Magnus said to

Beatle, loud enough for Toby to hear. "A whole lot of shots of him fucking it up. Like, shot after shot of him falling over, the bloopers reel. Whaddya think? You'd have plenty to choose from."

Beatle grinned. "Could be good."

But Beatle already knew what he was going to use for the opening credits. Winsome texting madly on her phone the beginning chorus bit of *Romeo and Juliet*:

2 h'holds, both a lyk in dignty,
In fair Verona, where we lay r scene,
Frm ancient grudge break 2 new mutiny,
Where civil blood makes civil hands unclean.
Frm 4th the fatal loins of these 2 foes
A pr of star-crost lovers t8 their life.

Toby kicked off and skated towards the steps, ollied up, turned one-eighty, went down the steps, had nailed it—but his weight was too far forward, and he stomped the board as he landed and snapped the deck. Again. But it was good enough. Beatle had caught enough of the landing for it to look as if Toby had done it right. He could edit out the stomp.

It had taken a million tries and three busted skateboards, but Toby had finally done the trick that was pivotal to the whole film.

Yes, sir, Beatle thought, the gods sure are smiling down on this golden boy at the moment.

*H*ope came into the kitchen and tossed some photos on the bench.

"Excuse-*moi*," she said, a teasing lilt in her voice. "Someone's got a secret admirer."

Destiny picked up the photos and flicked through them. There were three of them. One of her mom getting into her car. One of her mom checking herself in the rearview mirror. And one of her reversing out of the driveway.

"Where'd you get these?" Destiny asked, holding the photos between her thumb and forefinger as if there were something vaguely grubby about them.

Hope shrugged. "Mailbox."

"Where are they from?"

"Dunno," said Hope. "Mum, who took these shots of you?"

"What shots of me?"

Destiny's mom came over to the bench, wiped her

hands on her apron, and took the photos out of Destiny's hands. She frowned at them.

Then left the room, photos in hand.

*I*t's an oldie but a goodie: the black cat crossing your path, warning you that bad luck is about to wander into your life. Or is the black cat cursing you, causing bad luck? Whatever. A black cat crosses your path, you know you got to hold onto your hat; there's trouble a'coming.

But Beatle knew enough about black cats to know it wasn't always a bad sign. For example, if you happened to be a bride, and a black cat sneezed near you on your wedding day (what are the chances of that happening?), you'd have a happy married life. Or if a black cat walked towards you, it would bring good fortune—away from you, it takes the good luck with it. Fishermen's wives kept black cats while their hubbies were at sea, to stop danger from happening to their menfolk. In Ireland and Britain, apparently it's good luck if a black cat crosses your path, and bad luck if a white one does.

But as a general rule of thumb: black cat plus path plus crossing equals bad luck.

The fact is, a black cat crossed Beatle's path that

morning. And he wasn't happy about it.

Beatle stepped into the kitchen instead of heading into the bathroom for a shower.

"A black cat just crossed my path," he announced.

"I know. Isn't he cute?" said Winsome, her face crumpling into a smile at the mere thought of the black cat, harbinger of doom.

"What's he doing in here? Who is he? And no, he's not cute. He's a black cat, and he's just crossed my path, and you know what that means."

Winsome raised her eyes to the heavens.

"Oh don't be so ridiculous. You're such a girl. Black cats don't mean anything, and, anyway, for your information, owning a black cat is good luck."

"Except we don't own one."

"We do now."

Their mom called out from her bedroom.

"Beatle, darling, can you make me a cup of tea?"

You'd think their mother would be able to manage crawling out of bed before midday on a school day, but no. Who knew what time she actually slugged her way out of bed, but it certainly wasn't any time before 8:30 when he and Winsome left for school.

"I found him last night," Winsome continued, looking up briefly from her toast. "When I got home from . . . being out," out with Frank McCartney, obviously, "and I found him outside in the laundry. And he was stuck behind the washing machine, and looking so cute," she said, pouting her lips in what some people might consider a cute face, but which Beatle just wanted to smack, "so I brought him in, and he doesn't have a collar or anything, no tag, nothing, so I figure he's ours to keep."

Beatle chewed on his lip a moment, then turned and walked back out to the bathroom.

Now he wasn't sure. Owning a black cat was good luck. Having a black cat enter your home was no problem. Touching a black cat was a positive for your karma. So maybe it wasn't bad luck after all. Maybe it was a dose of good luck. Maybe instead of being a black-cat-crossing-his-path-bad-luck moment, it was a black-cat-now-lives-in-our-house-good-luck moment. Which, he had to admit, was how things seemed to be tumbling for him right now. Lady Luck was positively molesting him most days, his touch was so golden.

Beatle thought for a moment. It was a definite black-cat-now-lives-in-our-house type lucky event, he decided.

One more stroke of luck in a long, soothing massage of lucky strokes.

$\mathcal{L}$et's see how good your attention to detail is: Destiny's family has a dog called . . . come on people, you know this, she walked it in the park with Mathilde's ridiculously-named-dog, Fido. Destiny's family has a dog called . . . ten points if you said Pepsi.

They also have a cat called Puss.

They've had them both for four years.

Each night Puss goes for a wander around the neighborhood, probably slaughters a few native animals but hey, watcha gonna do, then saunters home at around 9:30, tucks herself into the U-shape made by Pepsi's belly and legs, and goes to sleep purring with happiness.

Sure, they say it's a dog's life, but it's not hell being a cat either, as far as Destiny could make out.

But on Tuesday night Puss deviated from her routine. She'd gone out to survey the neighborhood and snack on some tasty native treats, but she hadn't come back. Destiny had gone to the back door and called Puss in. She'd even played the dirty trick of calling out "dinner" when there was no dinner to be had, but still Puss was a no-show.

For four years Puss had gone out, wandered, and come home again.

A creature of habit.

Until last night. And she hadn't been seen since.

*Y*in has a yang. Black has white. And good luck has bad luck.

And the run of bad luck had started.

All because of a stupid black cat, crossing Beatle's path, inside his own apartment.

A stolen black cat, as it turned out.

Beatle knew it was all going to shit the next day when Destiny said to him, quietly, "Have you ever done anything really bad—something that's affected lots of people, not just you?"

They'd been sitting at the fish and chip shop on the corner of Glenferrie and Malvern Road, eating potato cakes, when her phone had rung. Her dad. She'd spoken to him in a low voice, turning her back towards Beatle so he couldn't hear, then after she'd hung up the phone she'd dropped this clanger about "Have you done anything bad?," relating to no part of their previous conversation whatsoever.

It had seemed a strange thing to ask, and Beatle had sat there trying to figure out where to go with it.

Finally, he grinned at her.

"Something really bad? It's my middle name, baby. Hard to know where to start."

And she'd smiled at him, but there was no crinkling around the eyes, no warmth spreading from her mouth to her cheeks. Only a sadness dulling her features.

Looking at her pretty face slumping opposite him, Beatle realized with a jolt that this was the moment to tell Destiny that he had a girlfriend; that he didn't know how things had gotten so messy and deceitful; that he hadn't meant to be an asshole, but that's how things had worked out. That he wanted to be with Destiny, but he didn't know how to break up with his girlfriend. That it's hard to break up with your girlfriend when she's also your sister's best friend. And goes to the same school as you. And you're going to have to see her every day for the rest of the year, whether she's speaking to you or not. And she's starring in your film as Juliet. And it's all very tricky and sticky.

He looked across at Destiny. He wasn't sure how he was going to tell her the truth, which words he was going to use and in what order, but he knew he was going to tell her because it was the only way forward.

But as he started to form words inside his mouth, as he was about to push them out, letter by letter, into this brave new world he was creating, he realized Destiny already knew. Ever since she'd stepped off the tram at Glenferrie Road, she'd seemed different from how she usually was. There hadn't been that same vibrant something that usually underlined each of her words.

That's why she'd asked him about bad things he'd done—as a test. To gauge on a sliding scale of one to ten exactly his level of slime. To see whether, when a huge gaping opportunity presented itself, he took it.

He looked down at his feet, ashamed.

"You want to talk about bad things I've done?" he said eventually. He took a deep breath, about to launch his confession.

"Well, actually," she said, tiredly pushing her hair off her face, "I was thinking more of something bad I've done."

"Something bad you've done?" he said, tucking her hair behind her ear so he could see her face better. "Impossible."

Destiny fumbled with her fingers, clearly unnerved by what she was about to tell him.

"Hey," he said gently, bringing her face around to his. "What's the matter?"

"Our cat's gone missing," she said. And then she shook her head. "No, that's not it. Our cat's been stolen, and it's all my fault."

"Your cat?" Beatle said, his stomach sinking fast until

it was resting on the seat under him.

"The thing is," she said, a breathy rush under her words, "we've got a stalker. Someone's been calling our house and hanging up. Stealing underwear. Leaving photos they've taken of us in the mailbox. And now the cat's gone. She's been missing since Tuesday night, and Faith especially is devastated because she was given Puss by an old boyfriend for her birthday, and now Puss has been stolen and it's all my fault."

Beatle's mind was lurching inside his head as if he had vertigo.

"Your cat?" he said dumbly, as if maybe that part of it was wrong. Maybe she meant her dog, or her rabbit, or her bird. Something else, anything else, just not her cat.

Destiny nodded.

"Yeah. And the whole thing is my fault," Destiny said. "Dad's been really freaked out these last couple of weeks, especially once we found the photos in the mailbox, and he told me to make sure I sealed the cat flap and not let Puss go wandering, but I forgot because I was working on this thing for my art project, and now we can't find Puss anywhere and Dad's really angry with me, and if he knew how much of it was my fault, he'd completely freak."

The guy came from behind the counter and cleared up a bit, stopping the conversation for a moment.

Winsome had stolen their bloody cat, thought Beatle.

She'd completely lost it. What the fuck was she doing? Calling McCartney's place. Taking his cat. Stealing underwear—that was particularly bizarre.

Although this would not be altogether out of character. Beatle remembered when they were at Elwood Primary, and Winsome had torn her spelling book in half, in front of the teacher, in front of the classroom. Simply tore the book up and let it fall to the ground at her feet. Beatle would never forget it. Everyone in the class had watched silently, then waited for the inevitable explosion from Miss Kerrison. His mom had been called up to the school, and there'd been a big hoo-ha about it; "No one's ever done anything like this before" and "We don't know if she can stay here if this is the way she's going to behave" and "This is absolutely unacceptable." And Beatle had sat in the foyer outside the principal's office and listened as his mom explained that "I don't know what gets into her sometimes" and "They don't see their dad much, maybe that has something to do with it" and "Maybe something happened with one of the other children that upset her."

But it was none of that.

Beatle had asked Winsome why she did it, that night, after they'd gone to bed. Winsome had turned over to face him as she lay in her bed with a broad grin and said, "I just wanted to see what would happen."

Simple as that.

"But I don't get it," Beatle had pressed. "I thought you liked spelling?"

"I do like spelling."

"You don't like Miss Kerrison?"

"Miss Kerrison? Yeah. She's nice. I just felt like ripping up the book. That's all."

And Winsome had rolled over to her other side and gone to sleep. The sleep of the innocent.

"None of us are allowed to be home alone at the moment," Destiny continued. "Mum's freaking out, Dad's spoken to the police, and now he's continually calling us to make sure we've gotten to school or work or whatever—that's why he called just now, checking up on me—and it's all my fault."

Winsome had stolen a cat, some underwear, was taking creepy photos, and making anonymous phone calls.

It was official. She'd lost it.

And now, somehow, Beatle was going to have to fix it all.

$\mathcal{B}$eatle's mom had taken him for a drive that Sunday afternoon when he got back from fish and chips and stalkers and underwear. He hadn't really wanted to, had been distracted after what Destiny had told him about her cat, but his mom was going down to Southland, which was quite a good drive, and he needed to get his hours up if he was going to try for his license in the next few months, so he'd agreed to go with her.

They'd been crossing Brighton Road, going down Glen Eira, when a car coming from the opposite direction turned right, straight into them, at thirty, maybe forty, an hour.

The thunder of metal on metal was sky shaking, signalling more dark storm clouds on the horizon for Beatle.

The impact smashed up the hood and mangled the driver's door so badly that Beatle could only get out by wedging his way through the passenger side door after his mom.

Beatle's mom rubbed her hand over her eyes. She looked older and fleshier around the face, as if the accident had dislodged her bones and her cheeks were now sunk down to her chin, dragging her eyes down with them.

"Look at the car," she said. "What a mess."

Beatle felt anger rising in his throat. He'd had maybe eighty hours of driving practice and having a guy smash into him wasn't what he needed right now. This guy had deliberately, and carefully, driven his car straight into them.

It was completely unbelievable. The car was probably totalled. Who knew how this would affect Beatle getting his license? "Any accidents, young man?" "Well, yeah. Totalled my mum's car." "Oh. I'm afraid you won't be eligible for your license in that case."

"What the fuck did you do that for?" Beatle said, stamping over to the other driver.

"Sorry. I didn't even see you," the guy said, staring numbly at the wreck that used to be his car.

"You didn't see us? How could you not see us? We're in a car. It's quite large. It'd be hard to miss us." And Beatle looked at his mom's car, which was all smashed in at the front. "Actually, you didn't miss us at all. You got us fair and square."

"I'm sorry," the guy said again.

Unbelievable.

"I just don't get how you could do this," Beatle said.

"Beatle. He didn't do it deliberately," his mom said, coming up behind him.

How could she be so reasonable? Beatle felt his fist clenching up. He turned to his mom.

"But that's the thing. He *did* do it deliberately. He deliberately turned straight into the front of your car. If he'd waited half a second longer before he turned, he would have driven straight into my door. I could be dead now. He's a moron."

"Beatle. It was an accident."

"Actually, I think you were going faster than you should have been through the intersection," the guy said. "Especially seeing as you're a new driver. If you'd been going a bit more slowly, you would have been able to stop, instead of driving into me."

"What?" Beatle said, turning slowly around to face the guy. Unsure that he'd heard correctly. "Omigod. What?" he repeated.

"Beatle. Leave it," his mom said. "Call the tow truck."

"What the fuck do you mean, I was driving too fast? I was driving at normal speed, and you drove straight into us. What? Am I not supposed to drive at the normal speed? Is that what you think? Just because I'm younger doesn't make this my fault."

"Well, if you weren't driving so fast, you would have been able to brake in time."

"Brake in time? Oh my fucking god."

"Beatle. Forget it," his mom said, holding onto his arm.

"I shouldn't have to be able to brake in time," Beatle said, shaking his mom's hand off his arm, "because you shouldn't have been turning into our car, dickhead."

His mom grabbed his arm again.

"That's enough," she said firmly, using a tone of voice Beatle rarely heard.

"It's not up to me to stop," Beatle went on, his voice getting louder and words spitting sharply out of his mouth. "It's up to you to wait until we've driven past, and then turn," he said. "When the way is clear," he added.

His mouth kept going, and he knew he was behaving badly, but he couldn't help himself. At least, he probably *could* have helped it, he probably *could* have stopped, but he didn't *want* to help it. It felt good. It felt great to be yelling at this guy in the middle of the intersection, and to be feeling justified in doing it.

Really fantastic.

It was like he was exploding, anger going in all directions, and he was loving it. All the mess in his life with Cilla and Destiny, Winsome and the cat, even general shit at school, and this guy was here in front of him, ready to be dumped on.

Beatle could feel his hand dangling at the end of his arm. It would be so easy to reach out and jab this guy in his stupid face. Punch some sense into him.

"I should drive slowly through an intersection," Beatle said, "so that if some idiot fuckwit dickhead like you happens to decide to turn into me, I can brake in time?"

"That's what safe drivers do. Yes," the guy said tightly.

"How would you know?" Beatle said, his voice rising. "How would you know what safe drivers do when you've just driven headfirst into our car?"

"Beatle," his mom said, dragging him towards the footpath, "there's no point."

"Yeah," Beatle said, "there is a point. The point is to get this guy to admit he was in the wrong."

"Beatle," his mom said, looking fierce. "Leave it."

And suddenly he didn't feel angry anymore. Just like that, within a moment, he felt completely exhausted. Blank. Nothing.

There's a joke about the balloon boy who has a

balloon mom and a balloon dad and he goes to a balloon school with balloon friends and a balloon principal. And one day, the balloon boy decides to take a pin to his balloon school, which is, of course, a disaster. And he's called into the balloon principal's office, and the balloon principal tells him, "You've let me down, you've let your school down, you've let your parents down, you've let your friends down. But most importantly, you've let yourself down."

And that's exactly how Beatle felt at that particular moment. Like a deflated balloon boy who's let everyone down.

He deflated down onto the footpath next to the road and watched the traffic slowly percolating past his mom's mashed-up car. His mom sat down next to him. The other guy went and sat in his car. Just sat there with his hands on the steering wheel, as if he were driving, except his car wasn't going anywhere.

Beatle's mom turned to look at Beatle, her forehead resting on the knuckles of her hand.

"What's going on, Beatle?"

Beatle shrugged. "Nothing."

His mom turned her wrist one way, then the other, then tapped at her jangly bracelet so that it moved to a more comfortable spot on her arm.

"They say senior year's a very stressful time," she said.

"Yeah. S'pose."

His mom examined a couple of the charms on her bracelet.

"Is it just senior year that's giving you grief? Or something else?" she asked.

"No. Nothing. I overreacted, that's all. I don't know. Getting smashed into when you're practicing driving is a pretty bad experience."

His mom nodded.

"Hmm. You know what?" she said, still looking at her bracelet. "If there's something going on that you'd like to talk about, you know you can talk to me, don't you? You and Winsome—"

"Yeah. Whatever. There's nothing going on."

"Okay."

She looked over and smiled at him.

"You know, when you were born—"

Beatle clicked his tongue. "Jesus, Mum, I'm not in the mood to be told I looked like a skinned rabbit again. I just don't find it that comforting."

"I wasn't going to talk about you looking like a skinned rabbit," she said. "Although, really, you did. All pink, with shiny skin and—"

"*Mum.*"

"Kidding. I was going to tell you about when my friend Robyn came in to see me."

Beatle looked out at the road, watching the cars go past.

"I mean, lots of people came in to see me," she went on, "and they were all very worried, and everyone asked how you were and how I was and how 'the baby' was— you know, Winsome—and whether there was anything they could do for me, and it was a pretty hard time. And then, this one day, this friend of mine Robyn came in, who I don't see very often. And she had a bottle of champagne in her hand, and she said, 'I'm here to celebrate,' and I said, 'What are you celebrating?,' and she looked at me as if I was mad and said, 'I'm here to celebrate the fact that you've had a baby.'"

Beatle's mom fiddled with her bracelet and looked at a patch of road.

"And I said to her that you were actually quite sick— I mean the doctors didn't even know if you were going to survive, and if you did survive there was a fair chance you were going to have some disability or other—and she said to me that if things didn't go well, she'd come and bring a bottle of scotch to drown our sorrows, but at the moment, things were okay, and she was here to celebrate with me. And it was the loveliest thing, because you know what, until that moment, no one had said congratulations. They'd all been really somber and worried and anxious, and she was the only one who came in and celebrated the fact that one of my twins was out in the world and that was something worth breaking out the champagne for."

Beatle nodded, his elbows resting on his knees and his hands dangling like hams.

"My point is," said his mom, "life throws up lots of stuff at you; you've already had more than your fair share for an eighteen-year-old—but as life goes on, you're going to have other hard times. And the hard times are good in their own way, too. Because the only way you can achieve true happiness is if you experience true sadness as well. It's all about light and shade. Balance. The sad stuff is just as important as the good stuff, because it gives you a chance to examine what's going on in your life, and what you want to change. If you're going through a hard time, just sit and think. And be grateful that you're going through a hard time, because hard times are what help you reach the next level of happiness."

"Mmm-hmm," said Beatle, staring at his hands.

His mom watched him a moment.

"I mean," she said, "take, for example, your stroke. I know it's not something you would have chosen to go through, but a lot of positives came out of it."

"Yep. I'm positive I hate my limp. That's one positive." She smiled at him. He didn't smile back.

"It made you who you are today."

"A freak who can't walk properly."

"A lovely boy who has more compassion than a lot of other people, especially most teenagers I know. You showed real strength of character to deal with it so well. And it showed you who your friends were, who you could rely on," no points for guessing she was referring to Cilla here, "and I doubt you would have even started thinking about going to film school if you hadn't had your stroke. You were too busy not taking life seriously to even think about what you wanted to do in the future. So a lot of good things came out of your stroke. And not just for you—for Winsome and Toby and all your friends. Cilla. I look at the lot of you and think you all changed after your stroke. It gave you all a sense of the importance of living for the day. It's not the ideal way to find out how fragile life really is, and what you want to do in life, and who your friends are, but it served its purpose. Without too many long-term repercussions."

Beatle didn't answer.

A tow truck drove up and a big guy hauled himself by his gorilla arms out of the cabin. He puffed up his cheeks as he came over to them. He looked over at the stack of traffic waiting to get past their two mangled cars.

"Well," he said, "you've made a real mess of things, haven't you?"

Beatle looked down at his fist, dangling from his arm.

"Yep," he said. "You're not wrong there."

*T*he cat was curled up on her lap while she watched the TV. Beatle felt a fury washing over him.

"Have you put an ad up for that cat?" he asked. "Tried to find its real owner?"

Sarcasm dripped over the words "real owner."

Winsome glanced up at him, then back at the TV.

"Nuh."

Beatle chewed on his mouth, trying to stop his words from exploding in her face.

"Well, don't you think you should? It's someone's cat. Someone owns that cat. You've had it for a few days now. Maybe it's time to give it back."

Winsome showed him her bored expression.

"I can't give her back. I don't know where she's from."

"Yeah. Right."

"What's your problem?" she said.

"You found it? In our laundry? Not in someone's front yard, for example?"

"Oh my god. That car accident's done something to

your brain. You've actually lost your mind."

"You're the one with the stolen cat, and I'm the one who's lost my mind?"

"She's not stolen," Winsome said, her voice raised. "Jesus. What's up your ass?"

"That cat's not ours. You've got to give it back to whoever owns it."

"I don't know who owns her. That's why she's still here. Am I speaking too fast for you? What part of 'I don't know who owns her' is confusing for you?"

Beatle glared at her. "The 'I don't know who owns her' part."

"Seriously," Winsome said. "You're really boring me. I didn't steal her. I found her. Different thing."

And then she stood up, holding the cat in her arms.

"I'm going to do some homework," she said. "And I'm taking my 'stolen' as in 'not stolen' cat with me."

To: ange398@hotmail.com.au
From: waltzingmathilde@hotmail.com.au
Date: March 12
Subject: Stalker ad
Dear Ange398,

We're the girls who replied to your stalker ad. We came around to your place a few weeks ago in February, but never saw you. Were you there? Did you see us? We met a guy who lived across the road from the address you gave us, but he said only an old man and his son lived there. He said the son's name was Angelo, but we were under the impression you were Angela. Maybe we got our wires crossed. Maybe we went to the wrong place. Just wondering if we had it right or not.

From
Destiny, Mathilde, and Netta

To: waltzingmathilde@hotmail.com.au
From: ange398@hotmail.com.au
Date: March 12
Subject: Re: Stalker ad
:)

To: ange398@hotmail.com.au
From: waltzingmathilde@hotmail.com.au
Date: March 12
Subject: Re: Re: Stalker ad
So does that mean we had it right or wrong? Are you Angela or Angelo?

To: waltzingmathilde@hotmail.com.au
From: ange398@hotmail.com.au
Date: March 12
Subject: Re: Re: Re: Stalker ad
:(

To: ange398@hotmail.com.au
From: waltzingmathilde@hotmail.com.au
Date: March 12
Subject: Re: Re: Re: Re: Stalker ad
Sorry, but the symbols you're sending through are a bit confusing. Can you be a bit clearer? We're just wondering whether we had the right address. Did you see us sitting out in front of your place? Were we at the right house?

To: waltzingmathilde@hotmail.com.au
From: ange398@hotmail.com.au
Date: March 12
Subject: Re: Re: Re: Re: Re: Stalker ad
-:

To: ange398@hotmail.com.au
From: waltzingmathilde@hotmail.com.au
Date: March 12
Subject: Re: Re: Re: Re: Re: Re: Stalker ad
??? What does that symbol stand for?

To: waltzingmathilde@hotmail.com.au
From: ange398@hotmail.com.au
Date: March 12
Subject: Stalker ad

Come off it. You look like smart girls—I'm sure you can guess what -: stands for. No? Won't even hazard a guess? Let me make it easy for you then. This :) is a happy face. This :(is a sad face. And this -: is the erection I've got right now, just talking to you.

Yes, I watched you out the front of my house but I couldn't come outside because I was preoccupied, if you know what I mean. The three of you looked so sweet, sitting out in front of my place, waiting for something to happen. Well, guess what? Something's happening.

Don't pretend you didn't know what would happen when you wrote to me. You replied to a "stalker wanted" ad, didn't you? Well, I'm the stalker you wanted.

I'm not sure which of you I followed, but whichever one it was, you live in a nice house, don't you? Big and impressive, with the pool out the back and the tennis court to the side. Saw your pretty mom getting into her swanky car the other day—hope you like the shot I took. And I'm not sure whose panties I got, but gee, they smell good and make me think of all three of you. I've called you a few times too. I'm not sure if you've noticed. Every few hours, just checking in to make sure you don't forget me. Pretty easy getting your phone number—can you imagine how I did it? I won't tell you now—I'll save that for later, when we know each other better.

Anyway, nice talking to you. Looking forward to seeing you again.

As for your cat. She's well and safe and happy here with me—I've just borrowed her to remind me of you. I'll return her later.

See you soon (although you might not see me).
Ange

*T*hey typed "Stalker" into Google.

22,200,000 sites came up.

According to Wikipedia, under "Psychology and Behaviors," there isn't your one standard stalker; there are a variety of stalkers. They can be divvied up into: the Rejected Stalker, someone who wants to get revenge after being divorced, separated, or maybe losing their job. Next are the Resentful Stalkers, a group who are angry and want to get revenge on their victim by frightening them. Then you have your Intimacy Seekers, looking for an "intimate, loving relationship" in all the wrong places. To them, their victim is their soul mate and they're "meant" to be together—if only they told their victim that. The next category is the scarily named Eroto-manic Stalker. They believe their victim is in love with them, reinterpreting any negatives from their victim into positives to suit the fairy-tale story going on inside their very own heads. The next category, the Incompetent Suitor, sounds like a harmless doofus, but has a fixation and belief that they are entitled to a relationship with their victim, like it or not.

"And finally," said Mathilde, scrolling down the page, "we have your Predatory Stalker, who will spy on the victim in order to prepare and plan an attack—usually sexual—on the victim."

Destiny frowned at Mathilde.

"And you read that out to me because . . . ?"

"Well, clearly to make you feel more attractive," said Mathilde. And then, seeing Destiny's unsmiling face, said, "Sorry. Joking."

"You have to tell your parents," said Netta. "This guy's obviously one of those Predatory Stalkers. You've got to tell your mum and dad. Doesn't matter if they're going to kill you. He might really try to kill you. Or rape you. You've got to tell them."

"We know where he lives," said Mathilde. "The police can handle it."

"And we can show them his e-mails," Netta added, tapping the screen of the computer.

Mathilde put her arm around Destiny's shoulder and gave her a squeeze, then jabbed at the computer screen, her pointer finger and thumb making a gun.

"You're going down, mister," she said, pulling her trigger finger down. "Bang."

"It's straight to jail for you, you dirty old perve," said

Netta. "You sure picked the wrong girls to mess with."

"He's going to rue the day he replied to our e-mail," added Mathilde.

The three girls looked at each other. The day he replied to *their* e-mail. They'd invited this creep into their lives, simply because they were a little bit bored during art.

Yep, Destiny's parents were going to kill her.

"I'll tell them," she said. "I'll tell them tomorrow night."

"Why not tonight?" asked Netta.

"Oh. I'm just not in the mood to be hung, drawn, and quartered tonight. I want to remain intact for one more night before I hand myself over to the executioners. Watch a bit of TV. Live a bit more of my life before they kill me."

Destiny looked back at the Wikipedia page.

"For tomorrow," she said grimly, "I die."

*H*ere is a list of the things that kept Beatle awake that Thursday night the twelfth of March:

#1: His sister had stolen a cat.

#2: A black cat who had single-handedly sucked all the good luck out of his life with one waltz through the living room.

#3: A black cat who had an owner frantically worried about her whereabouts.

#4: A black cat who, even if it wasn't actually physically driving, was certainly responsible for the smash-up-derby that had formerly been known as his mom's car.

#5: A black cat who Beatle was holding personally responsible for the loss of his calculator—his $230 calculator—that had been stolen out of his locker that very morning.

#6: A black cat who had frozen his computer this afternoon while he was editing the magnificent ollie that Toby had landed, causing all footage of that incredible stunt to be lost from his computer forever.

#7: Tomorrow was Friday the 13th.

Yep, Beatle's luck had officially turned. Like a milk-shake left out in the sun too long.

*H*ere is a list of things that kept Destiny awake that Thursday night the twelfth of March:

#1: She had a stalker.

#2: A stalker who she had e-mailed and actually invited into their lives.

#3: Her parents were going to kill her.

#4: Kill.

#5: Dead.

*H*ere's the deal: Top Arts is an exhibition that is held at the Ian Potter Gallery in Fed Square each year. The top final-year art students have their work exhibited for a few months, and it's open to the public.

Last year, six of the girls from Destiny's school were short-listed and had their work shown.

It's a very big deal.

And this Friday afternoon, the thirteenth of March, Mr. Castles had said very quietly, just a word in Destiny's ear when she brought her project up to his desk, "If you keep going the way you are, you'll be in Top Arts for sure."

Destiny had looked at him with wide eyes.

"The work you're putting in," he told Destiny, "the different ideas you're exploring, the way you keep hammering away at different thoughts, teasing them until you're satisfied—really, I'm very pleased with how you're coming along, and I'm looking forward to seeing your final pieces."

"Wow," Destiny said, a thrill zinging in her stomach. "So, you really think I might get in?"

Mr. Castles nodded.

"Absolutely," he said. "Look, it's early days yet, but if you keep going this way, you'll definitely be on the long list at least. The thing that you seem to get, that so many others don't, is your project is the place where you experiment, try different things, get things wrong, make mistakes. Say here, for example," and he opened to the page where she'd starting working on her tapestry, "you had this idea to incorporate the tapestry into your work. And you'd already pulled it apart a bit and made it a bit, um, grungy. So you knew which direction you were headed. Then here you've started experimenting with sewing the tapestry onto the canvas and painting around it. Which is fine. But then you start looking at different ways of using it: rolling it up, painting over it, pulling out every second stitch, experimenting with the way you're going to attach it to the canvas, sewing, sticky-taping, stapling. But then here," and he turned the page, "you've really started playing with the idea of what Home might mean. At first it's pretty predictable—house, chimney, garden, whatever—but then you've started looking at more macabre scenarios, which is where it gets interesting. Sinister men hiding behind trees, lingerie on clotheslines. It's unsettling.

Such a contrast to the tapestry. I find with girls—and I know I'm generalizing here—but often girls like to draw pretty pictures. Or they'll do something confronting in a sexual way. But they don't often do things that are grim and . . ."

"Depressing?" Destiny asked, feeling depressed that her work was so depressing, but exhilarated at the same time that Mr. Castles thought it might be selected for Top Arts.

"Threatening. And that's what makes it interesting. It's like that saying about families, you know, all happy families are the same, but unhappy families are all unhappy in their own ways. You know what I mean?"

"You think my family's unhappy?" she asked, that depressed feeling settling in her stomach.

Mr. Castles shrugged.

"I don't know. It doesn't matter. I don't care if your family's unhappy or the Brady Bunch. What I care about is the work you're producing, and at the moment it's looking brave and strong. And from what I know of what's been selected before, I'd say you're a shoo-in. So long as you keep going, pushing the boundaries."

"You think it might hang in Fed Square?"

"Exactly. And everyone can go and see it. Everyone. And I'll tell you something: there's no better feeling than watching people look at your work when you're exhibiting."

And that's when Destiny felt a definite sick feeling coming over her.

"Everyone?" she asked. "Just anyone?"

"Yeah."

"Neighbors, and everyone?"

"Anyone you like."

And here lay the problem.

Mrs. Sheffield would probably come, being the interfering old bag she was, and see her tapestry, and have a conniption on the spot.

Her mom would definitely come, and see the tapestry, and probably put two and two together, and have a conniption on the spot.

Mr. Boots, or whatever his name was, the local member of parliament, might come.

And have a conniption on the spot.

The police would come.

And have a conniption on the spot.

The security guard who was now regularly patrolling Mrs. Sheffield's place would come.

And have a conniption on the spot.

So, if Destiny's work was exhibited in Top Arts, she would be killed. By Mrs. Sheffield. By her mom. By her local member of parliament. By the police. And by the security guard.

There was only one thing to do.

She had to ruin her project.

"**Y**ou can't be serious," said Hope, sitting cross-legged on her bed and resting her back against the wall. "You're going to dumb down your project, because you don't want the old bat from next door to see you've got her tapestry?"

"I don't have any other option."

"But how bad are you going to be? How crap is your work going to be? Terrible? Bad? Average?"

"I don't know. Bad, I suppose. Average. I don't know. It just can't be that good."

"God," said Hope. "What a terrible mess you're in. Your teacher's told you your work's so good you're going to have to make it bad on purpose."

It seemed to Destiny that Hope had quite a sarcastic tone to her voice.

"You don't need to be all sarcasmic about it," Destiny said, wishing she'd never brought the whole thing up. Sarcasmic. Ridicamous. Absorootmee. They had a whole code of words that weren't to be found in the dictionary.

Hope shook her head.

"No. You're right. Poor you. So talented, yet having to subvert your talent because of Mrs. Sheffield."

"Piss off. I'm not saying I'm 'so talented.' I was just telling you what Mr. Castles said. Sorry I mentioned it. I thought maybe, I don't know why, I had this crazy idea that being my sister, you might be interested. But if you're going to go sarcasmic on me, forget I mentioned it."

Hope shook her head again.

"Well, I'm sorry if I think you're being pathetic. And kind of bragging at the same time. Like, 'I could get into Top Arts, but I'm going to make sure I don't.' I mean, seriously, I didn't realize you were such a loser."

"Omigod. What is your problem?"

"It just shits me. You're good at art, and now you're going to try not to do well in the one thing you're good at, because of Mrs. Sheffield. Get a grip."

"Well, what do you suggest? Mum will kill me, and if she doesn't, Mrs. Sheffield will. I told you, it was done by Spencer Tracy's wife, or something—the tapestry—some king or other."

Plus, there was the other matter of being responsible for the stalker and being killed for that as well. Destiny wasn't sure what the limit was, but she was pretty sure if you got theoretically killed enough times, there was a fair chance you would actually die.

Hope plumped up her pillow and leaned back against it.

"Just tell Mum," she said and shrugged. "I mean, she'll kill you, but so what?"

"Mrs. Sheffield will kill me as well."

"Yeah, probably," agreed Hope. "And after they've both killed you, you can move on. It's only a tapestry, for god's sake."

"Done by a queen," Destiny pointed out. "You forgot that part."

"Doesn't matter. Go down and talk to Mum about it. She'll be fine. And if she tells Mrs. Sheffield, you'll just have to deal with it. You're getting yourself all in a knot, but remember that book?"

"What book?"

"You know, my book on choice theory."

It was one of Hope's psychology books that Destiny had picked up off the bedroom floor the other night and read from cover to cover. *Choice Theory—The Alternative Therapy* by Dr. William Glasser, MD. Choice theory proposes that everything in life—absolutely everything—is a choice. Even being mad is a choice. If you don't want to be mad, you simply stop. If you don't want to have, say, obsessive-compulsive disorder, then just stop doing the obsessive-compulsive things you do. If you want to be more confident, then simply choose to be more confident. It's a strikingly simple theory, and as soon as Destiny had read it, she knew that she and Dr. William Glasser, MD were on the same page.

"It's the same thing with this tapestry," Hope said. "You can choose to blow your art project, or try as hard as you can and maybe, and remember it's only a maybe at the moment, get into Top Arts." Hope folded her arms across her chest. "It's your choice. And it's a no-brainer, so far as I can see."

Destiny propped a leg up and started rubbing her hand over her shin, checking how long the hairs on her legs were. There's something disgusting *and* satisfying about the hairs on your legs getting that bit too long. Kind of mesmerizing in how gross they can be. Destiny's were right on the edge of being gross, and definitely needed a shave.

"But what will Mrs. Sheffield do?" she said finally. "Mum will make me tell her for sure."

Hope shrugged.

"Dunno. She's the one who should feel ashamed, anyway, harassing her ex-daughter-in-law like that. I mean, have you heard what she's been doing to the poor woman? Calling her, demanding the tapestry back, just because the old bat had a hunch she'd taken it."

"Well, kind of because that's what Mathilde and I said," Destiny admitted.

"Oh, that's right. Yeah. What'd you say that for?"

"We were trying to get the heat off us. We didn't know her ex-daughter-in-law drove a blue Land Rover, or whatever it is."

Hope grabbed a hank of her long blonde hair and started tying it into a loose braid.

"You'll just have to take it on the chin," she concluded, clinching the end of her braid with a rubber band. "Tell Mum. Tell Mrs. Sheffield. Let her go ballistic at you, if she wants. But don't mess up your art project just because you don't want to get into trouble. I mean, it's pathetic. And in the end, you'll probably feel better for getting it off your chest."

Destiny thought for a moment, chewing the inside of her cheek. And then she swung her legs off the bed and went downstairs.

*D*estiny sat at the kitchen bench, watching her mom.

"Mum?" she said.

Her mom turned around.

"Yeah?"

"Um. I've got something to tell you."

"Okay." Her mom nodded and looked at her.

Destiny chewed on her lip. It wasn't going to be easy to get these words out. She looked out the window and watched the wind whirling in the trees, shaking the leaves as if trying to liberate them from the slavery of their branches. It was getting dark earlier now, and a tinge of coldness was bordering both ends of the day.

"Well?" her mom asked. "Spit it out."

"Hmm. Yeah, it's just that, I've got some good news, and some bad news."

A cliché. But clichés are only clichés because they work so goddamn well.

"That's good," said her mom. "And bad." She smiled.

"Exactly," said Destiny.

And then she didn't say anything.

"The phrase 'pulling teeth' occurs to me at this moment," said her mom, still smiling.

"Yeah, well, pulling teeth would be preferable," said Destiny.

"What is it?" asked her mom, starting to look concerned.

"Hmm. I'm just not sure how to tell you."

"Well, what's the good news? Tell me about that."

"Okay. Yeah, that's a good idea. Today Mr. Castles told me he wouldn't be surprised if my project gets into Top Arts."

Her mom smiled again, this time a wide grin that brightened her face. She came over and gave Destiny a hug and a kiss on the top of her head.

"Well done. That's brilliant. Congratulations."

"I mean, it's not definite or anything, because it's so early in the year, but yeah, he thinks the way it's coming along, I'll definitely be long-listed at the very least."

"So that's the good news?"

"Yeah."

"Okay."

And then Destiny didn't say anything.

"Oh, come on, Destiny," said her mom. "What can be

so hard? Just tell me. Once I know what the problem is, I know how to respond. At the moment, I'm not sure if I should be starting to feel angry or sick or worried. Is this something to do with the stalker?"

"Ah," said Destiny. "No. Although I have to talk to you about that, too. No, this is about my art project. The thing is, the piece that Mr. Castles is getting really excited about is a multimedia piece. A montage. It uses other materials, not just paint."

"Right."

"It uses a . . . tapestry."

"Oh," said her mom, a frown starting to muddy her features.

"One I found a few weeks ago."

"Right."

"One I thought was being thrown out."

"One attached to a chair?" her mom said, the frown starting to settle between her eyebrows and around her mouth.

"Yeah."

And then Destiny didn't say anything, because there really wasn't anything to add. Her mom took a deep breath, opened her mouth, then clamped it shut. Then opened it again.

"You took Mrs. Sheffield's tapestry?"

"Well, sort of, yeah," Destiny said, ducking her head.

Not that she expected her mom to hit her, but she knew what was going to hit the fan and she was trying to get out of the way.

"The one done by Wallis Simpson?"

"Yeah."

Her mom shook her head.

"Well, you'll have to give it back. I don't care if it was going to get you into Top Arts. That's tough luck. You'll have to give it back to her."

Destiny cleared her throat.

"I don't think she'll want it."

"Why not?"

"Well, it's not the same anymore."

"What do you mean?"

"It's kind of, um . . ." Hard to describe really. Wrecked? Ruined? Annihilated? "Changed."

"What have you done to it?"

"Well, first of all I cut out the word 'home,' to make it look a bit grungier and kind of, you know."

"You cut it?" her mom asked, her mouth pulling in as if her cheekbones had collapsed.

"And then I pulled out bits of it."

Destiny's mom ran her tongue over her teeth. Not a good sign.

"The one done by Wallis Simpson? You destroyed it?"

"Well, no, I didn't destroy it. I mean, I don't think it's

wrecked. I think it looks good, cool, you know. But yeah, she might not be all that happy with it."

Destiny's mom put her hand to her forehead, then turned away from Destiny and walked out without saying another word.

Hope came into the kitchen, sidling past their mom as she left the room.

"How did it go?" Hope asked.

"Not so bad, I suppose. All things considered. I suspect she's waiting until Dad gets home, and then she'll let it rip. So far, I'd have to say it hasn't made me feel a whole lot better, but it's done now, so I'll just have to deal with it."

As for the stalker . . . Maybe she'd leave that on the back burner for a while longer.

And then their doorbell rang.

Destiny and Hope went to answer it.

Standing there, ominously, was a security guard.

And standing beside him was Beatle.

*T*wo women—identical—sit on chairs facing the camera.

"I grew up in Melbourne."

"I grew up in Brisbane."

"I went to college and studied to be a dentist."

"I studied to be a dental hygienist."

"I got married at twenty-one."

The other one grinned.

"I got married at twenty-one."

"I've got three children: Zac, Molly, and Iris."

"I've got three kids as well: Zac, Milly, and Iris."

"I didn't know I had a twin until three years ago, when my mum finally told me."

"Three years ago my dad told me."

"We spoke on the phone a few times, and then arranged to meet at the halfway mark—Sydney—a couple of weeks later."

"The weekend before, my husband flew me to Hobart

as a surprise for a couple of days. He thought it would be nice to take my mind off waiting to meet her." The speaker tipped her head in the direction of her twin.

"My husband had the same idea. Flew me down to Hobart that weekend. So that's where we ended up meeting. The luggage carousel at Hobart Airport. The most surreal moment in my entire life."

They both crossed their legs, in the same direction, at exactly the same time. As they were crossing their legs, they both noticed, and started laughing. The same braying haw of a donkey.

Exactly the same.

"Sometimes," one of the twins said, after they'd finished laughing, "your destiny's your destiny and when the time comes it's going to happen, ready or not."

*W*insome walked into the living room all dressed in black. Black skinny pants, a black top, and black flip-flops.

"Where are you going?" Beatle asked, looking up from his math book, which was propped on his lap as he sat in front of the TV. Not able to answer any of the questions because his calculator had been stolen out of his locker yesterday morning. Damn black cat.

"Out," Winsome said.

"Where?"

"I'm going to see a movie. Don't know if you've heard of it; it's called *None of Your Business*. Adapted from that book—you might have read it—called *Get a Life*. Supposed to be really good—had some great reviews."

"Where's your ski mask?" Beatle asked.

"What?"

"You look like you're going to rob someone," he said.

She squinted at him.

"Yeah, a gas station," she said, walking into the kitchen.

"Just gonna roll a couple of guys, get some cashola, and make a night of it."

Beatle stayed on the couch but leaned over to see into the kitchen. Their mom was sitting at the table working on a chart while Winsome put the kettle on.

"You seeing your boyfriend?" he called out.

And heard—with some satisfaction—their mom say to Winsome, "You didn't tell me you had a boyfriend."

Winsome walked back into the living room, shooting daggers at Beatle.

"I didn't tell you I have a boyfriend because I don't have one," she said over her shoulder. "I think Beatle lost his marbles when he crashed your car," she added, doing the looping crazy signal with her finger.

"So where are you off to?" their mom asked, coming into the living room and leaning against the doorjamb.

"I'm going out. To Cilla's," Winsome said.

Their mom stared at Beatle.

"But what about you?" she asked him. "Why aren't you going to Cilla's?"

"I'm not going to Cilla's," Beatle explained to his mom, "because Cilla is only allowed out one night a weekend now—her dad's come down on her hard to study—and we're going out tomorrow night."

He'd spoken to Cilla when he'd gotten home. She'd sounded sad and quiet, but when he'd said he might come around to see her, she'd said he wasn't allowed. She was staying at home and not doing much; she'd see him tomorrow night.

Beatle looked at Winsome. There was no way she was going to Cilla's.

"In fact," he added, happy to get Winsome in deeper, "it's weird that you're allowed to go over to Cilla's place seeing as her dad's gone all psycho-strict. Are you going to do some English homework?"

With an emphasis on "English."

Winsome glared at him.

"No. I'm going around to talk to her because she's having problems with her boyfriend, who's being an asshole to her." Beatle felt their mom look at him, but he kept eyeballing Winsome. "I'm going around to comfort her. Personally, I think she should dump him. He's not worth the aggravation, but who am I to say?"

Their mom looked at the two of them, said nothing, then went back into the kitchen. Winsome left the apartment and slammed the door shut.

Beatle remained on the couch, staring at his math homework but not actually reading it. Winsome wasn't going 'round to Cilla's place—he'd lay money on it. She was going out with Frank McCartney.

Fine. Whatever. He picked up his pen to start tackling problem number two.

But something nagged at him about Winsome and McCartney. Something didn't make sense. If McCartney was her boyfriend, then why had she stolen his cat? And the underwear—that was weird. And the photo. The calling and hanging up Beatle could understand—she'd call, then hang up if Frank didn't answer. But the rest of it didn't gel.

Especially the cat.

Why had she taken the cat?

Unless. . . . Beatle thought back over the past three weeks at school. He'd noticed that McCartney had seemed a bit cool towards Winsome. Wasn't being as chummy with her in class as before.

At the beginning of the year, the dynamic between Winsome and McCartney in class had been blazing. She'd been happy to answer questions; he'd single her out and ask her what her opinion was on some text or other; once Beatle had realized they'd hooked up, all their classroom antics looked a whole lot less like enthusiastic student-teacher relations and a whole lot more like your standard flirting.

In front of twenty-five other students.

But these past few weeks—ever since Beatle had caught them in the car—things had definitely cooled. Winsome wasn't putting her hand up in class, she wasn't offering her opinions about the themes and issues, and

McCartney was skipping over her, barely noticing her.

And even after class, in the quad or generally around, Beatle hadn't seen them together.

And suddenly, Beatle had it: motive.

There's no crime without motive, and now Beatle had one. Winsome had been stealing stuff from Frank's place because he'd dumped her. She'd obviously told him that Beatle had caught them together, and he'd gotten cold feet and pulled the plug on the whole deal.

And Winsome hadn't liked it.

She'd never been dumped before. Always the dumper, never the dumpee. So now she was after revenge.

What was that saying their mom often spouted? *Hell hath no fury like a woman scorned.*

Frank McCartney had scorned Winsome.

And now she was madder than hell.

$\mathcal{B}$eatle dialed Winsome's phone. He'd talk to her—tell her he'd guessed. Say McCartney had mentioned something to him at school today about his missing cat, and Beatle had put two and two together. He'd tell her that if Frank didn't want to be with her anymore, she'd have to deal with it. That's what everyone else did. Not go completely psycho and start stealing his sister's underwear and the family cat.

He heard her cell ringing in her bedroom.

Shit. She'd left her phone at home.

New plan.

He'd call Cilla. Check whether Winsome really was there, or if she was really on her way to the McCartneys' place to steal more stuff.

But Cilla was evasive.

"Um, she's not here yet, but yeah, she's coming over and we're just going to hang out."

And it made Beatle sad that things had crumbled between him and Cilla to the point that she was now quite happy to lie to him for Winsome's sake.

Never mind that he had spent the past month happy to lie to her for Destiny's sake.

Of course, Cilla wouldn't realize Winsome was stealing underwear and cats. Cilla would never condone something like that. Winsome had probably told her she was meeting up with McCartney and needed Cilla to cover for her. But still, the fact remained that when it got down to the wire, Cilla would lie to Beatle for Winsome. Lie to her own boyfriend to protect her best friend. Said a lot about which relationship she valued more.

"Hey, Cilla," Beatle said, feeling all sad and regretful. Regretting how he'd been taking his guilty conscience out on her. "I'm sorry I've been shitty lately. I think, you know, senior year, it's pretty crazy. And I'm just being an asshole."

"It's okay," she said quietly. "Don't worry about it. We can talk about it tomorrow night. Forget it."

"Okay. Hey, Cilla."

"Yeah?"

"Is Winsome really coming around to your place?"

"Yeah."

"What about her and McCartney?"

"Oh."

Ever since he'd found out about McCartney, he'd been waiting for Cilla to mention it to him. He knew Winsome would have told her that Beatle had caught them, but Cilla hadn't said a word. Just kept mum about the whole deal. So this was the first time he'd actually put into words that he knew. He heard Cilla cough slightly, as if clearing the way for the words to get through.

"Well, look, yeah," she said. "I've been waiting for you to mention it to me, but you haven't, which is not really that much of a surprise considering how things seem to be going between us, but, anyway, I don't want you to start asking me what's going on with her and Frank, and what I think about it and stuff, because she's my friend, and you're my boyfriend, and it makes it tough for me if I'm stuck in the middle. It's her choice and her decision, and I really can't talk to you about it, because I feel I'd be betraying her. Do you know what I mean?"

Beatle raised his eyes to his bedroom ceiling. Yeah, he knew what she meant. What she meant was, she was in tight with his family, best friends with his sister, and he should never have started going out with her in the first place.

You don't just break up with your sister's best friend and think everything's going to work out all right.

"So she's definitely coming 'round to you then, is she?" he asked.

"Yeah. She should be here any minute."

"Hmm. Okay. Well, I'll see you tomorrow night."

And he hung up the phone. Knowing full well that Winsome wasn't going around to Cilla's place. She'd left a good fifteen minutes ago. She'd definitely be at Cilla's by now if that's where she'd been headed.

There was only one thing to do.

Despite the fact that it was Friday the 13th.

He was going to follow her.

Stop her.

Explain to her why what she was doing was so wrong.

He grabbed the piece of paper on which Destiny had written her address and phone number the other day.

Then walked out the door.

*I*t was windy outside Destiny's house. Autumn was starting to take its job seriously and whip the leaves out of the trees.

Beatle plunged his hands into his pockets and tried to decide what to do. He knew he couldn't stand out on the footpath for too long, otherwise he'd look suspicious. If any of the neighbors saw him, they'd definitely think he was dodgy. Especially if they'd heard there was a stalker in the area—they'd be onto him like a shot. He couldn't just stand outside waiting for Winsome to come out, but he wasn't sure where else he was supposed to go. He was new to this whole "casing someone's joint" business.

He looked up at the house. It was a big double-story place. The huge wooden front door was framed by stained-glass panels. A gigantic tree stood sentry out front, its branches waving like a warning to him in the yard. There were lights on downstairs, and a couple of lights on upstairs, but all the blinds were drawn, so he couldn't see inside. He walked down the street a little, past the house, trying to spot Winsome in the garden, but it was pretty difficult to see anything. It was dark, and with her all-black number, she'd be hard to make out.

"Winsome," he spat into the front garden, but the wind snatched her name away the minute it came out.

"Winsome," he called again, but he knew there wasn't a chance she'd hear it.

Even if he yelled like a foghorn, she wouldn't hear him. She could easily be there looking at him, and he wouldn't have a clue. Although he knew that if she were in the front garden looking at him, she'd have come straight out and asked him "what the fuck" he was doing there.

He knew that about her for sure.

He looked around to check that no one was watching him, then sidestepped neatly through the gate and into Destiny's front yard. One good thing about it being windy and dark: If he couldn't see properly, no one else could either. So if anyone came out the front door of Destiny's place, he'd be able to hide without too much grief, behind a tree or something.

He squatted down and started moving through the garden, hugging close to the trees. The side gate was open, and Beatle noticed the reflection of the lights inside the house shining onto a pool out the back. Beatle felt sure that the gate wouldn't normally be left open. It just didn't look like that sort of a house. It looked like the sort of house where gates would be pulled shut behind you and the trash bins would sit neatly behind a discreet fence, waiting to be emptied.

He snuck up to the side gate and peeked through. He still couldn't see anything, and it occurred to him that maybe Winsome wasn't here after all. I mean, if you were a stalker, you wouldn't go on a stalking mission every night. Even psychopathic stalkers had to take the occasional night off.

It was easier to see in the backyard because the entire back of the house had no blinds. Floor-to-ceiling windows opened on to the back, so the light from the house spilled over the trees, reflected off the pool, and added a warmth to the garden. From his position, Beatle could see into the kitchen, and he saw Destiny sitting on a stool, talking to an older woman, obviously her mom. Destiny was wearing an old, ragged-looking pair of sweatpants that hung off her hips. Her dark hair was pulled back in a ponytail, and she had her flip-flops dangling from her toes. The slightest movement would have made them fall to the floor.

And that's when Beatle heard a voice behind him.

And the voice was saying, "What the fuck are you doing here?"

When the security guard nabbed Beatle in the garden, Beatle started explaining to him in urgent whispers, "This isn't what it looks like. I'm not perving on them; I'm looking for my sister. She's supposed to be here." And the security guard had given him a greasy look and said, "Is that your sister? That one you're staring at?"

Beatle had looked back at Destiny, sitting at the breakfast bar talking to her mom, and for a split second he considered saying yes. If he said yes, the guy would let him go and Destiny would never know. But he couldn't. He couldn't say yes. Besides, she looked nothing like him. He'd never have grown on a tree with such a gorgeous branch.

"No," he said, all the air going out of his lungs.

"Didn't think so," said the guard. "What's your name?"

Beatle looked at him.

"John Lennon."

The guard looked at Beatle.

"You're in big trouble, fella. Don't make it worse."

"That's my name," Beatle said, opening his hands to show what an honest citizen he was. "My mum's a big fan."

The guard glared at him, pencil poised.

"It's really my name," Beatle said.

Finally, the guard scratched it onto the paper.

"Address?"

Beatle shook his head. "Look. Do we really have to do this? It's not how it looks. I promise."

"Never is. Address?"

Beatle gave it to him.

"You live on your own?"

Beatle stared at the guard.

"I'm in high school."

"You live on your own?" the guard repeated.

"No. I live with my mum and my sister."

"Phone?"

"Yes. We have one."

"I'm telling you," the guard said, wagging the pencil in Beatle's face, "this is a serious matter. Don't make things worse by being a smart-ass."

Beatle told him his number.

And then the guard hauled Beatle's smart-ass up to the front door for Destiny to find on her welcome mat, like a paper bag with a steaming turd inside.

A couple of weeks earlier, Frank McCartney had brought a polygraph machine into class.

He'd plonked it down on his desk, grinning, and said, "So, who's game?"

Everyone in the class looked at him blankly. Not being altogether familiar with lie detectors, none of them knew what it was. So no one was game.

McCartney looked around the room, his grin getting bigger, as he said, "It's a lie detector. So come on, volunteers?"

A resounding silence.

Beatle, for one, had no intention of plugging himself into a lie detector for Destiny's brother in front of the whole class. No way, no how.

Eventually Toby said, "What have you brought that in for?" and McCartney leaned against his desk, folded his arms across his body, and said, "I've heard that some of you have been cheating on your tests. So," and he smacked his hand onto the machine, "I've brought this little baby in to find out who."

Jaws dropped onto desks.

And then McCartney laughed.

"Kidding. Actually, I got this off a friend and thought it might be handy for demonstrating to each of you the physiology of emotion."

Again, jaws dropped, but this time it was because they didn't know what the hell he was talking about.

"I'm sorry," Nique said, putting up her hand, "but can we have that in English? This is, after all, an English class."

"I mean," McCartney explained, "the actual physical responses that happen in your body when you experience an emotion. In this case, a negative emotion. The emotion of deception. Does anyone know how this thing works?" he asked, tapping the machine.

No one answered. They were all sure it was some kind of weird trick question, and none of them wanted to get stuck being McCartney's guinea pig for a lie detector test.

Especially not Beatle.

"It checks out your blood pressure, your breathing, and how sweaty you get when you're asked certain questions. You know, when you're asked a normal question, your body responds in a certain way that you can't control. And then, when you get asked a question that you don't want to answer, or that you are going to have to lie about, your body responds in a different way. So, who wants to have a go?"

No one's hand shot up.

McCartney grinned at them some more.

"Don't worry," McCartney said. "I'm not going to ask about cheating. I'm just going to ask a few questions, and we'll be able to see how you respond."

"But, Mr. McCartney . . ." Nique said again, her hand going up.

And McCartney clapped.

"Our first volunteer. Great. Well done. Come on up."

"Oh, but hang on," Nique spluttered. "I was just wanting—"

The class started clapping, too, applauding that someone else had gotten roped into the whole deal.

"Come on," McCartney said. "It'll be fine. I'll just ask you some basic questions. The point is: you've got a creative writing piece coming up in the next couple of weeks, and when you're writing it, I want you to think about the physical responses a character goes through when something stressful occurs in his or her life. We all know about theme and entertaining the reader and whatever. But I want you to start *really* writing, *really* experiencing what's going on in the character's life. Remember I read you that bit out of *Due Preparations for the Plague*? And the physical responses of the characters? Remember how that made you feel? You understood the anguish, the terror the characters were experiencing. Your own heart rates increased—remember, some of you said that—simply because the author had explained the physical reactions so brilliantly."

McCartney had told Nique she'd be going "on the box." Apparently, that's the term used for undergoing a polygraph test.

Now, standing on the front doorstep of Destiny's house, Beatle felt sure that if he'd been "on the box" at this particular moment, the needle on the graph would have been going crazy, showing his heart beating a gazillion times a minute, his breathing shallow and abrupt and catching in his chest, and his fingertips positively dripping with sweat.

Destiny and one of her sisters—who seemed the polar opposite of Destiny, with long blonde hair in a braid down her back and fair skin—stood there staring. Until Destiny finally said, "Beatle. What are you doing here?"

And didn't sound altogether thrilled to see him.

The security guard didn't seem surprised when he said, "You know this fellow?"

Destiny frowned and nodded, and her sister curled her lip and said, "*This* is Beatle?"

Well, that had to be a good sign—Destiny had mentioned him to her sister.

The security guard said, "I think you'd best get your parents," and Destiny said, "Oh, okay" and turned to walk up the stairs, leaving her sister standing in the doorway, watching Beatle.

If Beatle were writing an essay for McCartney's class, he'd have described how his heart was going *boom boom boom*, and his palms felt hot and clammy.

He'd have written that it reminded him a bit of when he had his stroke, and he vaguely wondered whether he might collapse right here, right now, and let someone else clean up the mess. For the first time in his life, having a stroke seemed the preferable option. The inside of his mouth was making an extraordinarily squishy noise every time he swallowed, and even his breathing seemed to be all ostentatious and "Listen to *moi*, listen to *moi*, listen to the way I blow out like an angry wild animal, and then when I breathe back in, listen to how thunderously loud it sounds."

And then Destiny's sister said, "Aw-kward," and walked up the stairs, too.

Leaving Beatle on the front doorstep with his new best friend, Mr. Security Guard.

$\mathcal{B}$eatle's mom had a theory about rich people:

"They might be rich," she'd say, "but they're not happy. Everyone's got their problems, and in a funny way, you're lucky if you don't have much money because you can worry about being broke, and be happy with everything else in your life. You know, you can be happy with your children and your friends and the fact that it's a sunny day, because they're all things that are good in your life. But if you're rich, you don't have the luxury of worrying about money, so instead you have to worry about other things, and find fault with things, like your husband and your children and your friends, and sue people who have annoyed you or stepped on your toes, and you know it's a fact that most rich people are on antidepressants, don't you?"

Probably not a fact, exactly, but something his mom was happy to bandy about whenever the mood took her.

And now, here was Beatle, giving these rich people one more thing to worry about.

Beatle could tell them the truth. Lay it all out in front of them: "Winsome—my sister—is having an affair with Frank—your son, your brother. Which would be fine, except he's also her English teacher. And you know what? I don't really care, but the fact is, Winsome is best friends with my girlfriend, Cilla, which complicates things somewhat. But it seems Mr. McCartney's dumped her, anyway, so now she's calling your place, and stealing underwear and your cat—it's back at our place—and I came around tonight to tell her to lay off the weird-ass behavior, but she's not here, so no harm done then, eh? I'll be off home. See you 'round."

Clearly the truth wasn't an option.

Destiny came back down the stairs with her mom following behind her, and her sister, and a younger brother.

"Hi?" the mom said, a questioning sort of hello, as if she weren't sure it was quite the appropriate word, but she wasn't sure what else to use. "What's going on?"

The security guard pushed his shoulders back and jutted his chin out.

"I found this young man in your garden, spying on you and your daughter in the kitchen," he said.

"Oh," said Destiny's mom, her hand flying up to her neck, checking that he hadn't stolen something straight off her very own body while she wasn't looking. "Um, come in," she said, leading them into the room at the front of the house.

"I'll just make a couple of phone calls and then I'll come in, if that's all right with you, ma'am," the guard said, as if world safety rested on his shoulders.

Destiny's mom nodded and showed Beatle through the door.

It was a comfy room, with dark floorboards and a shaggy white rug in the middle, and black bookcases lined with books and a couple of Chinese-y looking statues, and the fireplace was all painted white with a basket of pinecones inside it, and the couches were long and low and covered in a cream fabric which Beatle's mom would never have had in her house in a million years and all Beatle could think was, "Shit. Rich people and their lawyers. Great."

"So . . ." said Destiny's mom. "I'm confused. What were you doing in our garden?" she asked Beatle.

Beatle pressed his lips together. "Um . . . looking in the window."

"Oh," said Destiny's mom, her mouth turning down as if she'd eaten a pickled onion. "Looking in at us? In the kitchen?"

Beatle nodded.

"And so . . ." she looked like the whole thing was having trouble piercing her brain, "are you the one who's stolen the girls' things?"

Beatle groped around like a drunk man inside his mind for the right answer. He could deny deny deny; that was an option. But the truth was, the underwear was probably back at his place, and the cat was certainly there, and if they bothered coming around to his joint, which he was pretty sure Mr. Security Guard was going to recommend, then he was going to be dumped right in it, like it or not. He could explain to them that it was his sister's fault, but that seemed the coward's way out. And even if he didn't get on with Winsome all that well at the moment, he would always defend her to the end. She was his twin. They'd shared a womb. He wasn't going to start telling tales on her now.

Besides, if it came out that she was having an affair with her teacher, she might be expelled. It would wreck things for her. He couldn't do it.

So instead he nodded. Yes, he'd stolen the underwear.

"And our cat?" she asked.

Beatle nodded.

Destiny's mom wiped her hand over her face. Beatle didn't dare to look in Destiny's direction.

The security guard came into the room and stood to one side, watching.

"And you've been calling?" Mrs. McCartney asked Beatle. "And hanging up?"

Beatle nodded again.

And then no one said anything for a long time.

"Oh my god," Destiny's mom finally said, as if the facts had only now gotten through. She shook her head. "What is wrong with you?"

Beatle didn't answer.

"What are you doing this for?" she pressed him. "Do you have any idea how much trouble you could get in? Do you know how horrible it is for us, for our family, to be wondering what's going to happen next? Why someone's doing this to us? Where our cat is? Do you know how that feels? Do you have any idea?"

Beatle shook his head and looked firmly at a spot on the carpet.

"I mean, can you even vaguely comprehend how worried you've made us? Worried that someone's going to attack one of our girls? That none of them are safe? Even at home? Do you have any idea how sickening that is? To not feel safe in your own home? To not know whether you can keep your children safe?"

Beatle could only shake his head.

"I mean . . . I don't know what to do. Do we call the police? I suppose we have to."

The guard nodded.

"I think that's the way to go," he said. "An extremely valuable tapestry chair was stolen from the property next door a few weeks ago. That's why I was checking things out—the lady next door hired me to. This man's probably responsible for that as well."

Good. Great. The tapestry chair. Beatle remembered Destiny telling him all about it and their having a good laugh. It had been one of those funny getting-to-know-you stories, and now he was getting nailed for stealing that as well. He stared down at the floor, because really, what could he say? If he told them the truth, he'd be sinking Destiny in it. And if he denied it, they wouldn't believe him, anyway.

"Oh," said Mrs. McCartney, looking over at Destiny, "I think that's a different matter altogether. We need to talk to Mrs. Sheffield about that. Um, so, what do you normally do in this situation?" she asked the guard.

"Well," he said, adjusting his back so it was ramrod straight and jutting his chin out so that he looked like one of the four faces on the side of Mount Rushmore, "we should call the police, and I'd like to ask him about Mrs. Sheffield's item. Find out what he knows. If he's been taking things from here, there's a fair chance he's taken her chair as well."

Beatle shook his head harder.

Destiny's mom sighed.

"How old are you?" she asked Beatle.

Beatle looked up at Destiny's mom for the first time. Her head was tilted to the side, the way Destiny sometimes tipped her head, and her eyes looked kind of sad.

"Eighteen," Beatle mumbled.

"Eighteen," she echoed. "I mean, for god's sake, what were you thinking?"

Which was funny because it was exactly the same question Beatle was asking himself.

*T*ime is a tricky thing. Fluid. Ten minutes can barely fit into the time it takes to spit some days, but other times ten minutes plods along, heavy second by heavy second, each one lingering way past its use-by date.

Time—sitting in Destiny's living room—seemed to hang like gloopy air, suffocating Beatle with each tick of its tock. The one moment he wanted it to spin away like a top, time—being the perverse bastard it was—stood sullenly in the room like some unwanted fat cousin, refusing to budge.

Even classes didn't drag like this interminable illness that was Friday the 13th of March in Destiny's living room.

"My husband is on his way home," Mrs. McCartney said as she came back into the room. "He'd like to talk to you."

Beatle dropped his head.

Yep.

Great.

Exactly what he felt like. A chat with Destiny's dad.

The doorbell rang.

Destiny's mom got up to answer it.

Beatle sat there, staring at his hands, wanting to look at Destiny but not wanting to look at the same time. He was pretty sure he could imagine the expression she was wearing.

And that's when he heard them. The women's voices.

The women's voices that sounded scarily like his mom and his aunt.

"I hope you don't mind," the woman who sounded like his mom was saying, "but I've brought my sister along—this is my sister, Lally. . . ."

Shit.

Just when you think things can't get worse. . . .

$\mathcal{B}$eatle looked at his mom through Destiny's eyes.

Destiny's mom was glamorous and slim and wore nice clothes and frosted pink lipstick, while his mom was like a carnival refugee with her jingle-jangly earrings like mini-chandeliers hanging off her head and some kind of moo-moo type outfit, the sort of thing some people might unkindly describe as a "tent dress."

She came into the living room with Lally trailing in her wake like a boat. Lally, who was wearing her swirly green pants with the purple knitted top that looked completely normal when she was at home, but looked out of place when she wasn't.

"Darling," Beatle's mom said, striding across the room, not even having the good sense to notice how out of place she was and how loud she was being and looking in such a somber environment.

And then she leaned over and gave him a kiss.

Yes. You heard right. Gave him a kiss.

"Now, what's going on?" she said, plonking down next to him as if they were all friends here and there was nothing to be worried about. "I got a call from a security man," and at this, the guard stepped forward.

"That was me," he said. "I called you."

"Yes," Beatle's mom said, frowning, "and you said something about him being in someone's garden—is that right? But I'm not exactly sure what he was doing."

And here she looked at Beatle, as if he were going to help her out.

Beatle looked back down at the carpet.

"Apparently," Destiny's mom said, "your son has been stalking our daughter Destiny."

There was a pause, and then Beatle's mom said, "I'm sorry, what? Stalking your daughter?" She shook her head, her earrings making a cheap, jangly noise. "No, I don't think so. That doesn't sound like Beatle at all."

"Well, I'm sorry," Mrs. McCartney continued, "but we've been getting phone calls at all hours of the night, and we've had some underwear stolen . . ."

"No," said Beatle's mom.

". . . and he told us that he's taken our cat . . ."

"Your cat?" Beatle's mom said.

"The one that's at our place," Beatle mumbled.

"The little black one?" his mom asked.

Beatle nodded.

"A black cat?" Destiny's mom said. "No. That's not ours. Ours is a white fluffy thing."

Beatle looked up.

"Yours is white?" he said.

"Yes."

And then he looked back at the carpet. Because if anything, that made things worse. Winsome hadn't stolen their cat. She probably hadn't stolen the underwear either. Or made the calls. She hadn't done any of it.

So he'd come here, to be nabbed by security and dragged in front of Destiny's family and his mom and Lally for no good reason at all.

None.

And then his mom looked at him.

"But I'm confused," she said.

"I'll tell you later," he said.

The last thing he wanted was a conversation with his mom in front of Destiny's family about exactly what was going on.

"So the cat's not yours?" his mom continued.

"No," said Destiny's mom. "Not if it's black, it's not."

"So what's this business about stalking, then?" his mom asked.

"We'll talk about it later," Beatle repeated.

"Why would you be stalking this girl?" his mom went on. "What about Cilla?"

There.

She'd said it.

Great.

Thanks very much.

"Cilla?" Destiny's mom asked.

"Cilla," Beatle's mom explained, "Beatle's girlfriend. They've been together for years."

Beatle felt body-slammed as all the breath whammed out of his lungs.

Mum, your work here is done.

He slid his eyes over to see whether Destiny had heard. That last bit about him having a girlfriend, together for years. Destiny stood up and left the room.

Bumping past Frank McCartney as she left.

"Beatle?" McCartney said, coming into the living room. "What are you doing here?"

And he didn't sound altogether thrilled to see him.

"You know this boy?" Destiny's mom (also Frank's mom) asked.

"Yeah. I teach him," Frank said, staring at Beatle in what could only be described as a most unfriendly, unteacherly, unmentor-y way. "What are you doing here?"

"He was hiding in our garden," Destiny's mom said.

"In our garden?" McCartney echoed.

"He said he stole our cat," Destiny's mom said.

"You stole our cat?"

Beatle shook his head.

"At least," Destiny's mom put in, "he *said* he stole it, but it turns out that the cat he's talking about is a black cat not white. So clearly it isn't Puss."

"Clearly," said Frank. And then he gave Beatle a hard look. "Beatle. What's going on?"

Beatle looked around him.

In the living room—staring at him as if every word coming out of his mouth was going to explain it—were Frank McCartney, Destiny's mom, Destiny's sister with the blonde hair who looked like a photo negative of Destiny, a young guy who must have been Destiny's brother Ern, the security guard, Beatle's mom, and his aunt Lally.

All staring at him, waiting for answers.

And none of the answers he had were answers he wanted to give.

He looked at McCartney.

"Sir," he said, "can I speak to you a minute?"

"I think you'd better."

"In private?"

McCartney sighed. He stood up and nodded at Beatle. "Come into the kitchen."

Beatle followed him.

"What's this about, Beatle?" Frank said, leaning against the kitchen bench and folding his arms defensively across his chest. "Have you come to tell my parents about me and Winsome? Are you trying to blackmail me?"

Blackmail? If only it were that simple.

Beatle opened his mouth, but wasn't sure what to say. Not even now. Nothing was going to sound right.

"No," he said at last. "God, I came here because I thought she was stalking you. I thought she'd taken your cat. I knew your cat had been taken, and I thought Winsome had taken it."

"Why on earth would you think that?"

"Because you've split up with her. I thought she was mad at you."

"We haven't split up," Frank said softly.

Beatle looked at him.

"When Winsome told me you'd caught us, I thought it would be best if we laid low. Weren't so obvious. I could lose my job, you know."

Beatle nodded.

Frank looked down at his shoes.

"There's, you know, only six years difference between us," Frank went on. "She's eighteen years old. If we weren't at the same school, there wouldn't be a problem. So we've been cool towards each other. How did you know our cat had been stolen, anyway?"

Beatle chewed on his lip.

"Destiny told me," he said.

"Destiny? My sister?"

"Yeah."

"How do you know Destiny?"

"I met her a few weeks ago. Actually, a month ago exactly. Last Friday the 13th. And I've been seeing her ever since."

Frank looked at Beatle.

"But aren't you with Cilla?"

Beatle nodded glumly.

Frank laughed.

"Shit man," Frank said. "You've got yourself in a bit of a mess."

And then the doorbell rang again.

And they heard Frank's mom say, "Oh my god."

*S*tanding in the open front door, framed by the stained glass of the side panels, was the security guard with a man who looked to be in his thirties.

A man standing there with some kind of bald animal in his arms.

"I thought I heard something," said the guard, "so I went outside to check things out. I found him, and this." He held up a roll of duct tape. "I think he was going to tape the cat to the tree."

Beatle looked at the cat dangling from the man's arms. The cat that was bald as a skinned rabbit. Pink as a newborn.

*B*eatle, his mom, and Lally were walking to the door.

Frank had done a stellar job, Beatle had to admit. A magnificent tap dance, lots of noise, his hands moving, his feet knocking out a rhythm, all designed to stop them from asking too many questions.

"It's an assignment I gave the kids," Frank had said. "And I must say, I'm impressed with how well Beatle has done. I asked them to write about being arrested. Committing a crime. How it would feel. And Beatle thought that if he came here, he could experience the feelings, to give his work an authentic tone, without getting into too much trouble. He knew I was going to be home soon; he knew I'd be able to explain it to you. I mean, it's unorthodox, but I certainly think he'll be getting a very good grade for this project."

"He did it for an essay?" Destiny's mom said doubtfully.

Frank clapped Beatle on the shoulder.

"That's commitment," he said.

"Committed, more like it," Hope muttered loud enough for them all to hear.

And then, before he could chicken out, Beatle said, "Do you mind if I have a word with Destiny. Before I go?"

$\mathcal{B}$eatle and Destiny sat down on the front steps of her house.

"I've got a girlfriend," he said quietly.

"I figured," said Destiny.

"I was going to tell you last weekend when we were having fish and chips, but somehow, it just didn't come out."

Destiny picked at her fingernails, then stared across the front lawn, watching the tree maybe, or the houses across the road.

"I liked you as soon as I met you," said Beatle. "I like you a lot. But I like my girlfriend a lot, too. She's a great girl."

Destiny bit her lip, but didn't respond.

Beatle looked at her. This girl who usually spoke in a breathless, words-tumbling-out type way. Who had a laugh underlining everything she said. Who made him want to kiss her every time she opened her mouth. And here she was, mouth shut, not even looking at him.

"I got together with Cilla after I had my stroke," Beatle said.

Destiny flicked her gaze at him for a moment, straight into his eyes.

"That's why I limp," he said. "Nothing exciting. No Mafioso. Just a stupid, embarrassing stroke."

He shrugged.

"So I had this stroke, and when I was in the hospital, I got together with Cilla. And the only reason I called you that day and invited you to Chadstone was not to see you—I didn't want to see you, because I knew I couldn't resist you—but I had to see you because I wanted to make sure you didn't mention me to your brother."

"Nice," said Destiny.

"Because if you mentioned me to him," Beatle bulldozed on, "he'd mention it to my sister, and she'd tell my girlfriend and then I'd be done."

Destiny looked at him.

"Why would Frank bother telling your sister?"

Beatle hesitated a moment, then sighed.

"They've hooked up."

"This is your twin sister?" she asked.

"Yeah."

"But doesn't Frank teach her as well?"

Beatle nodded.

"And he's hooked up with her?" she clarified.

Beatle nodded again.

"Gee," she said, shaking her head. "Is this some family thing you've got going? Hook up with people you're not supposed to? You got a competition going or something? A bet riding on it? You and your sister trying to win some money off each other?"

There it was, that breathless, tumbling-words thing, but without the underlining laughter. Just a shitty, pissed-off, breathless tumbling.

"I'm just telling it like it is," Beatle said, knowing that what he was saying wasn't pretty.

Destiny shook her head.

"What an asshole," she said. Beatle nodded.

"No. I mean, really. I'm glad you've offloaded," she said. "I hope you feel better getting it off your chest. Should I thank you now or later?"

Destiny stood up and looked down at him.

"I can't believe I liked you," she said. "I thought you were funny and witty and cute and nice and interesting. And now I find out you're a fucking asshole."

Beatle ran his tongue over his lips. They felt dry and horrible, after all the awful things that had come out of them tonight.

"I am an asshole—you're right. A complete fucking asshole. But I'd still like to see you again."

Destiny laughed. A hard, scoffing noise.

"See me again?"

Beatle looked up at her.

"I know I'm an asshole," he went on. "I know this whole thing has been a disaster, but I really like you."

Destiny stared down at him, her mouth cold.

"What if I called you?" Beatle persisted.

"I doubt I'd answer."

And Destiny walked back inside, shutting the front door behind her.

*A*fter the humiliation of having Beatle's mom tell her entire family that Beatle's had a girlfriend "for years"; after the police took away that freak-show who'd tried to tape their cat to the tree; after the hands-down worst night of Destiny's entire life, her mom suggested they go see Mrs. Sheffield.

"Might as well get it over and done with," Destiny's mom said. "The night can't get any worse."

How wrong a mother can be.

When Mrs. Sheffield told them to come in—a stiff martini clasped in one of her crippled claws—her voice sounded slightly slurry, but that wasn't really much of a surprise considering it was eight o'clock at night and Mrs. Sheffield usually started drinking around five. On a good day.

They went into her living room with its musty, floral couches and carved wooden side tables and vases and lamps and fringing and rugs and long, heavy, floor-length curtains and statues and knickknacks and god only knew what else, and watched as Mrs. Sheffield settled herself into the chair in front of the TV—an arts and crafts woman yelling from the small screen about how to decoupage a wooden box—before seating themselves opposite on the floomfy couch that was under the window.

Mrs. Sheffield tipped a bit more martini down her throat, then looked across at Destiny's mom.

"We have something to tell you," Mrs. McCartney said, prodding Destiny with her elbow.

Destiny cleared her throat.

"Yes?" Mrs. Sheffield asked.

"Well, you know your tapestry chair . . ." Destiny said softly, hoping that maybe the volume of the television would prevent Mrs. Sheffield from hearing a word she said, ". . . I took it."

Mrs. Sheffield was taking the final swig of her martini as Destiny launched into her confession.

At the words ". . . I took it," the old lady gasped, swallowing the martini olive whole—pit and all—straight into her gullet. Her glass smashed to the floor, and Mrs. Sheffield launched herself at Destiny, grasping at her face as if to scratch the rest of the confession straight out of her mouth.

Destiny jumped up and squealed, clutching at her mom, while her mom bent over Mrs. Sheffield and swatted Destiny's hands away, telling her, "Stop it! What are you doing? She's choking," and grabbed the old lady from behind in a bear hug, pumping under her ribs in an effort to Heimlich-maneuver the olive out of her throat.

Destiny stood up on the couch as if she'd seen a mouse and watched as her mom kept pumping at Mrs. Sheffield's tiny, bony frame, imagining ribs cracking rhythmically in time to her mom's efforts.

"Get down from there," her mom snapped at Destiny. "Call an ambulance!"

Destiny jumped off the couch—carefully avoiding Mrs. Sheffield—and ran into the kitchen, figuring there was bound to be some sort of phone in there, but she couldn't find anything. Finally, in the hallway she found an old telephone—the sort with a rotary dial—on a dark wooden table near the front door. She picked up the receiver. At least it had a dial tone. And then she wasn't quite sure what to do. How did these phones work? She put her finger gingerly in a number hole and pushed it all the way around, as far as it would go, then watched the circular dial click back into place. Twice more she put her finger in a hole and dialed.

Surprisingly, it worked.

"Police. Fire. Ambulance," the operator said.

"Ambulance," Destiny said, her voice sounding panicked in her own ears. "Now. Right away. She's not breathing. She's an old lady."

She didn't mention the tapestry. Too much information.

After she hung up, she frowned. Her hand reached into the back pocket of her sweatpants—and pulled out her cell. The time she'd wasted looking around the house for a phone and . . . well, it just wasn't worth thinking about.

She ran back into the living room, where Mrs. Sheffield was now slumped on the floor with Destiny's mom kneeling beside her, both hands splayed over her chest and pushing hard down onto her lungs, exactly the way you see them do it on TV.

Destiny couldn't watch. Two old-lady legs were on full display, her dress was hiked up around her thighs, and a grayness seemed to be leaching from the leather of her shoes straight up her legs and into her face.

The ambulance got there within a couple of minutes. But not in time.

Mrs. Sheffield choked to death on her martini olive.

Destiny had killed Mrs. Sheffield.

On Friday the 13th of March.

As Destiny and her mom walked back home, her mom slung her arm around Destiny's shoulder and said, "It wasn't your fault, you know."

"Not my fault?" Destiny yelled. "Of course it was! The entire thing is my fault!"

Her mom shook her head.

"Darling," her mom's voice sounded like a prayer in church, "she probably didn't even hear what you said, she was choking before you even started, probably. It wasn't your fault. It was an accident."

But Destiny noticed that when they got home and her dad commented on how fortunate it was that they were there when she was choking . . .

"Even though you weren't able to save her," he said, hugging her mom to his chest and kissing her forehead, "at least you were with her in her final moments, trying to help. You did a good thing."

. . . that her mom didn't look at all convinced.

A guy and a girl sit on chairs, facing the camera.

"Our mum is a twin," says the girl, "born at 11:53 or whatever—p.m.—on the twenty-third of October. I only know this because she's told us about a billion times." The girl raises her eyes to the heavens. "And then her twin sister was born at 12:04 or something—a.m.—on the twenty-fourth of October. So even though they're identical twins, Mum's a Libran and our Aunty Lally is a Scorpio."

"But what's even freakier," adds her brother, "is the same thing happened to us."

"Beatle," the girl continues, and she tips her head in her brother's direction, "was born on the eighteenth of December, and I was born the next year on the first of February. So we're twins, but we're born on different days, in different months, in different years."

"There's forty-five days between us," her brother butts in, "and Mum thinks we've got this freaky forty-five day rule happening. Everything between us happens forty-five days apart."

"But that's only because Mum is a freakazoid about signs and coincidences and whatever, and is the sort of person who would find a coincidence in the most unco-incidental thing ever," the girl adds.

"I got my first tooth forty-five days before you," says her brother. "First word, first steps."

"According to Mum," his sister points out. "I mean, who's to know, but that's what she says. Personally, I don't remember."

"I got my appendix out, and then forty-five days later you were rushed to the hospital to get yours taken out," Beatle says.

"Yeah, that's true. That was pretty freaky."

"Forty-five days after I crack a joke, you finally get it," he says.

The girl sighs and shakes her head.

"Anyway, Beatle had a stroke about, what, three years ago," she says.

We hear the mumbled voice of a person off-camera.

"Yeah," the girl says. "Very unusual. But it does happen. Anyway, the night he had his stroke, I was over at my friend's place and I started feeling strange, nauseous. And then I vomited. I hadn't been drinking or anything. And then Magnus rang—Beatle's friend—to say something was wrong with Beatle. So my friend and I went over and Beatle's on the floor. Can't speak, can't walk, nothing. I mean, we've never had that twin-thing—experiencing the same thing at the same time—but yeah, that was pretty weird, that I started vomiting probably at the exact time that he had his stroke."

"And then?" Beatle says, looking at her significantly.

"Well," and the girl reluctantly nods, "then, he was in the hospital for a while, and in rehab, and got better—well, as better as he's ever going to get . . ."

Beatle thumps her. She rubs her shoulder, but looks satisfied that she's provoked a reaction.

". . . and he came home and everything was fine, back to normal, and then one morning, I went into the kitchen and fainted. And Mum freaked, because she thought I was having a stroke, same as Beatle."

"Forty-five days, exactly," Beatle adds, "after I'd had my stroke."

His sister nods.

"Yeah. That's true. Forty-five days after. But I think, maybe subconsciously, because Mum's always going on about this forty-five-day thing, I fainted because I knew it was forty-five days after he'd had his stroke. You know, the power of suggestion. So yeah, anyway, that's us. Twins, but born in different years, with this stupid forty-five-day rule that Mum thinks we've got happening."

"I've thought of another one, Win," Beatle says.

His sister looks at him.

"Forty-five days after you go in the bathroom, you finally come out," he says.

She shakes her head.

"Forty-five days after you start being annoying," she says back, "you finally stop." And then she hesitates. "Actually, that's not true," she decides. "You never stop being annoying."

He grins at her.

"No seriously," she adds. "Never."

"And everything is right with the world," Beatle says, grinning at the camera.

*M*ost years there is only one Friday the 13th. Occasionally there are two. Very rarely there are three.

This year, there were three:

Friday the 13th of February.

Friday the 13th of March.

And Friday the 13th of November.

Friday the 13th of March was the last time Beatle had seen Destiny. Watched her stand up and go inside—wind whipping the leaves on the dark trees—after she said to him, "I doubt I'd answer."

You remember. You were there.

Her hair was pulled back in a ponytail, straight off her face, and when she'd said "answer," that little lispy thing underlined the word. And then he'd felt a sting as if she'd slapped him when she shut the door.

Never to be seen again.

Not at the Espy, or the Morton Lane Bar, or Scream, or any of the other places they'd gone together. Nothing.

Nada. Zilch. One day she was in his life and in his head, and the next day, gone.

Just a memory.

Of course, things hadn't gone much better once he got home.

As soon as he'd walked through the front door with his mom and Lally, Winsome had come out from her bedroom, her cell phone in her hand, and wagged it in Beatle's face.

"Omigod," she said. "Are you serious?"

"What?" Beatle said, although he had a fair idea what she was referring to.

"Come in here," she said and pulled him by the arm into her bedroom and shut the door.

"Frank called me." She stared at Beatle as if seeing him for the first time. "I mean, seriously, you're certifiable. You thought I'd stolen their cat? And their underwear? I mean, gross. As for his sister," Winsome continued, "I mean, what about Cilla? You do remember you've got a girlfriend already, I hope."

Beatle sighed and plonked down on her bed.

And words came out of his mouth. Lots of words. Words about not being sure, and words about feeling that he was with Cilla but she wasn't necessarily the one for him, and words about the nagging feeling he had that she was an accidental girlfriend, and accidental girlfriends weren't the best kind.

And through it all, Winsome sat on the bed next to him, letting him talk.

It had felt good to get the words out. Like he'd used a can opener on his head, and all the thoughts that had been sloshing around inside, making it hurt, were now tipped onto Winsome's bedroom floor for the two of them to sift through and sort out.

"So what are you going to do?" Winsome had asked when he was done.

"I don't know. I mean, Destiny doesn't want to have anything to do with me, but you know, I think I should talk to Cilla, anyway. Maybe have some time apart."

"I didn't realize you felt such an obligation to stay with her," Winsome said softly.

"It's not an obligation exactly," Beatle said, "but yeah, it's tough if we break up, because she's your best friend. Does that mean she doesn't come over anymore? Will it be weird if she does? I don't know. But I really like Destiny—a lot—and the fact that I can be so into another girl, that must mean I shouldn't be with Cilla."

Winsome shook her head.

"No. You shouldn't. And you know what? Cilla's going to be devastated . . ."

"Thanks. That makes me feel better."

". . . but she'll get over it. She's crazy about you, but she doesn't want to be with you if you're not into her. And you know what else?"

"What?"

"She will survive without you. And my friendship with her won't change. And she'll still come over here and it might be awkward at first, but then we'll all get over it. So don't beat yourself up too much about breaking up with her. That's life," Winsome said, shrugging. "People break up. And people get over it."

And then she put her arm around Beatle and hugged him close to her.

"What about you and Frank?" Beatle asked.

"What about us?" Winsome said, pulling back.

"Are you going to keep seeing each other?"

Winsome puffed up her cheeks, then blew out.

"Dunno. We need to talk about it a bit more, but Frank was saying he thinks maybe we really should stop. I mean, seeing you at his place, he said he just felt sick if anyone found out about us. He doesn't want to lose his job. He might never be able to teach again. It's going to be hard, but I think we'll have to leave it for a while. At least till I graduate."

Breaking up with Cilla had been tough, but as Winsome had predicted, she got over it. And how. Since September, she'd been seeing this guy called 'Brocky and seemed startlingly happy.

"I told you she'd get over you," Winsome had teased him one day recently.

Yep, it sure looked like she was over him.

So now, here he was at Friday the 13th of November.

Eight months down the track.

Exams were finished, school was finished, he had his driver's license in his wallet, and next month he was starting college interviews.

And tonight he was going down to the George Cinema on Fitzroy Street, St Kilda, to the screening of a documentary called *Twin Thing*, which he and Winsome had been interviewed for earlier in the year.

Being involved in the documentary had been an opportunity for Beatle, seeing as he wanted to go to film school. The way the director had set up the cameras, positioned the lights, the different effects he'd created with different lenses, the way he'd dealt with his sound guy and the cameraman—Beatle had watched them as much as they'd watched him and used quite a few of their techniques in his version of *Romeo and Juliet*, which was finally finished, hallelujah to that.

So tonight was significant because he'd finished his short film and was seeing the final cut of the documentary.

But it was significant for another reason, too. Tonight

was Friday the 13th, and despite the facts and figures (*British Medical Journal*, remember? Fifty-two percent more accidents, remember? Actual, solid, verifiable facts, remember?), he'd planned to go out after the screening and have a big night.

Not such a big deal for most people, but a major step for Beatle.

Since Friday the 13th of March, he'd been making a concerted effort to give all his superstitions the old heave-ho.

If salt spilled on the table, he'd just wipe it into his hand and throw it in the trash instead of tossing it over his shoulder. He'd opened an umbrella inside the apartment one day, just for the heck of it. He'd even walked under a ladder, deliberately, and been none the worse for wear. He hadn't gone so far as to smash a mirror, but who wanted to test that theory and be landed with seven years' bad luck?

He didn't read horoscopes anymore and had banned his mom from reading them out to him. Admittedly, he continued reading the horoscopes in *Street* magazine, but that was completely different; that was more to keep an eye on Destiny Auroraborealis-Jones than anything else. Until one day when—just like that—her column stopped. No explanation. No "Thanks for the memories." One week, Destiny Auroraborealis-Jones, the next week, nothing. Just an ad plugging the lineup of bands at the Espy over the coming week to fill the gaping hole left by the lack of any column by Destiny Auroraborealis-Jones.

Over the following weeks Beatle had checked for her column, until he eventually realized it wasn't just a short break. That was it. She wasn't writing it anymore. His last tenuous link with Destiny was severed.

It had been a big moment. A final nail. Sad, because it meant he couldn't hear her voice anymore (even if it was only on paper). But good, because it signaled the end of all things superstitious and star-related. A change in his destiny, as it were.

Beatle sat down on his bed and jammed his feet into his laced-up shoes.

Progress, he thought to himself. He was making real progress.

$\mathcal{D}$estiny sat with her fingers hunched over her keyboard, waiting for inspiration to hit.

Nothing. Nada.

The cursor blinked expectantly as she stared at the horoscope and waited for her fingers to start punching some words—something, anything—onto the page.

LEO (Destiny)

So much had happened over the past few months since she'd written her last column: finishing high school for the rest of her life; getting short-listed for Top Arts; getting together with and then breaking up with a new guy, Gus—it was almost as if she had too much to write about.

So she did what she normally did when she was stuck.

She got up and went into the bathroom. Plucked her eyebrows. Got rid of a couple of strays. Looked at herself in the mirror. Smeared some Vaseline over her lips. Pushed her hair up on top of her head in a kind of messy bun to see how it looked. It seemed to Destiny that when she piled her hair up on her head with her hands it always looked better than when she used pins or clasps or whatever. She thought maybe it was worth trying to invent some kind of hair-thing that worked exactly the same as hands. Sure, there were those comb things that you squeezed open and clamped shut, but they were never exactly right—they always stuck out from your head, announcing to the world they were there. She wanted to invent something more subtle. Something that you combed through your hair like fingers, and when your hair was exactly how you wanted it, the thing just stayed put. Hair-hands, she'd call it. She wasn't sure who she should speak to about it but figured someone in her family would know someone who knew someone who would know exactly how to do it.

It couldn't be that hard.

She went back into her bedroom and wrote "hair-hands" on a scrap of paper, then turned back to face the blank page on the computer.

LEO (Destiny) was still on the screen with nothing written underneath it. Exactly as she'd left it before she went into the bathroom.

Destiny sat down and put her fingers in position, as if concentrating on the mechanics of typing would help get some words onto the page.

She looked at the computer screen.

LEO (Destiny)

Nothing.

LEO (Destiny)

This has been a big year for you, and next year's going to be even bigger.

Nuh. The word "lame" sprang to mind. That wasn't going to rock anyone's world. She pushed the delete button, watching the cursor move backwards. She looked at the blank screen. She pushed the apple key and the Z key, bringing back the words she'd just written. Easier to have some words and start fiddling with them than have nothing on the screen at all.

She needed to get on a roll.

So rather than stressing over Leo, she went on to the next one.

VIRGO (Ern)

This was an easy one. He wanted to stay home over the holidays while their parents went down to the beach—and there wasn't a hope in hell that was going to happen. She settled her fingers on the keyboard and started typing.

VIRGO (Ern)

Saturn might be in your house this month, but you won't be staying at our house without the folks over the holidays. You can dream, little buddy, but it ain't gonna happen.

There. Finished. One down, eleven to go. She tapped the "return" key and started on the next line.

LIBRA (Frank)

She knew exactly what she was going to write for him as well.

She remembered sitting at the kitchen bench with him the morning after that horrible Friday the 13th of March.

"Beatle said you've been going out with one of your students," she said. Her throat clamping at the mention of Beatle's name.

Frank looked at her, then nodded.

"Yep. I have."

For most people this wouldn't seem a major thing, but for Frank it was a revelation.

"And I really like her," he added. Not the type of thing that had ever come out of Frank's mouth in all of Destiny's years being his sister.

"So what are you going to do?" she asked.

Frank sighed.

"We've decided to stop seeing each other. She's going to ask to be transferred to another English class . . ."

"Oh."

"She's going to say she wants to switch so she can have two free periods in a row on a Tuesday and work on her pottery without being interrupted."

He looked down at his bowl, scooped the spoon through some cereal, then let the spoon drop against the rim, not even bothering to lift it to his mouth.

"Her not being in my class will make it easier," he said solemnly, "but I'm still going to be seeing her at school every day, and it's going to be hard. But I don't think we've got a choice."

He looked at Destiny.

"You know what? You'd really like her. She's a fantastic girl. Interesting. Smart. Witty. Funny. She's gorgeous."

He took a mouthful of cereal, then glanced across at Destiny.

"I'm sorry about Beatle, by the way," he said.

The second mention of Beatle's name. Destiny felt herself blush and put her hand up to her cheek to keep Frank from noticing.

"What's his girlfriend like?" she asked. The question she'd been wanting to ask Frank ever since she'd heard he had one. "You know her?"

"Cilla? Yeah. She's nice. Although I'd have to say they're a weird match. I remember the first time I heard they were together, I couldn't imagine it. But it sort of made sense. She's Winsome's best friend."

"Why aren't they a good match?"

Frank shrugged. "Cilla's very . . . earnest. She doesn't laugh much. She's smart, super-intelligent, and I don't know, Beatle seemed sort of too much of a guy for her. He's always mucking around, being a smart-ass, never taking anything too seriously, and she takes everything very seriously. I kind of figured that maybe opposites attract. But then," and he looked significantly at Destiny, "maybe not."

Frank had put his arm around Destiny's shoulders.

"Have you spoken to him?" he asked.

Destiny shook her head. "No. And I don't want to, either. Never again in my life."

The annoying thing was, eight months along, and not a single phone call. He hadn't even given her the opportunity to hang up on him. To tell him once more in no uncertain terms that she wanted nothing to do with him. That he was a bastard, and he had a girlfriend, and what was he doing kissing another girl, anyway, and she'd never be able to trust a guy like him, so there was no point in them ever seeing each other again, and don't ever call her again. Ever.

And then she would have hung up on him.

But he'd never called.

Not a word. Not even a missed call that could have been from him.

Nothing.

Which was good, especially seeing as she never wanted to speak to him again.

She propped her fingers back on her keyboard and started typing Frank's horoscope.

LIBRA (Frank)

As the planets circle the solar system, I'm pretty sure you're going to be circling one particular girl who caught your fancy a little while back. Good luck with it.

Actually, she was kind of looking forward to meeting Winsome. And dreading it at the same time. To be reminded of Beatle every time she looked at Winsome was not going to be a good thing, but she'd get over it.

She moved to the next horoscope.

SCORPIO (Prue)

Well, that was easy, too. So much had happened in Prue's life recently, Destiny decided to mention everything.

Congrats on the new job, the new boyfriend, and the new house. Looks like things are finally looking up for you.

Hmm. Things were starting to move a bit more quickly now. Like a well-oiled machine. Three down, nine to go.

SAGITTARIUS (Grace)

Now was a good time to mention to Gracie that she wanted to start writing the column again. She'd dropped it halfway through the year because she couldn't fit it in with her schoolwork, her art project, and her social life;

something had to give, and it was the column. But now that school was over, she had more time, and she sure could do with the money. Destiny thought for a moment. And then she decided the direct approach was always going to work best.

SAGITTARIUS (Grace)

With the Moon in Mercury, I thought it might be good to have me moonlighting for the magazine again. It was always a very popular column—remember?

Maybe not so popular, but certainly not unpopular, which is the main thing.

Next up was Capricorn. Her mom.

This was always the hardest column to write, because her mom didn't really do much except go for lunch, have a sneaky injection of Botox (and then deny deny deny), and cook dinner for the family. Destiny supposed she probably did other things, but it wasn't clear what those other things were.

Destiny always felt like the columns she wrote for Capricorns were a bit lame, but she wasn't quite sure how she could fix it.

Of course, she could refer to that whole business with Mrs. Sheffield, but even now, eight months later, she still wasn't over it herself.

Destiny looked at the computer screen.

CAPRICORN (Mom)

At Mrs. Sheffield's funeral, her son Antony got up and spoke to the congregation, mentioning how fortunate his mom had been to have such wonderful neighbors: "They were there with her, giving her comfort, wonderful people." And Destiny had sat staring at her lap, wishing she wasn't there.

CAPRICORN (Mom)

I know you want me to come down to the beach house for the entire holidays, but I can't. All my friends are in Melbourne. And yes, Ern, it is completely different. I'm eighteen, you're not. Deal with it.

Simple.

Noncommittal. No reference to Mrs. Sheffield.

The only good thing that had come out of the whole disaster with Mrs. Sheffield was when Destiny overheard Antony telling his brother after the funeral, "At least we don't have to worry about the chair anymore. It was awful. Susan can have it, as far as I'm concerned," and his brother had clinked his glass and said, "Amen to that."

Destiny pressed the "return" key and started on Aquarius. Then Pisces, Aries, Taurus, and Gemini—they were all easy to write. Stuff about finishing school, opening new shops, and stopping cracking corny jokes (that one for her dad because really, he had to stop).

And then she got to Cancer.

Hope.

This was a particularly nice one to write, although it also raised some unpleasant memories of that terrible night on Friday the 13th of March.

CANCER (Hope)

Venus (being the planet of love) has well and truly moved into your house, and looks like it's not budging for a long time. Maybe a certain handsome police officer has it under house arrest.

As it turns out, good things do come out of bad situations. Officer Ed is one example. Tall, handsome, and funny. And in charge of the stalking case regarding Angelo Degustino. And smitten with Hope.

Angelo had gotten ten months in jail.

Hope had gotten twenty dates, so far.

And Destiny had gotten into thirty billion times more trouble than she'd ever been in before in her entire life, for having behaved so stupidly and answering a "Stalker Wanted" ad.

She leaned back from her computer and scrolled through what she'd written. Yep, it was all coming together. She just needed to write the last one. Hers.

LEO (Destiny)

This has been a big year for you, and next year's going to be even bigger.

She still wasn't sure what to write.

She didn't want to put in anything about being

shortlisted for Top Arts, because she didn't want to brag.

She didn't want to write about the whole bust-up with Gus, even though that was topical. But it seemed mean to use him for fodder for a magazine, especially since she knew he was still pretty cut up about the split.

And she didn't want to write about school being finished, because she felt like that part of her life was over and not worth mentioning.

She sat looking at the screen for a moment. Tapped her fingers on the keyboard, as if impatiently waiting for the Leo forecast to arrive so she could type it in.

And then she smiled to herself. Erased what she had written. Started typing. It was short. It didn't need to say much. And it was a cliché. But what it said was exactly how she felt at this moment.

LEO (Destiny)

Today is the first day of the rest of your life.

*F*riday the 13th of November.

An officially un-superstitious Beatle sat in the back of the cinema with Toby, Magnus, Lindy, Andrew, Sally, and Tim. Stragglers came in, looking for seats, as the lights dimmed slightly. Winsome, Angie, and Nique walked past, trying to find three seats together.

Noah, the director, stood up on the stage at the front of the theater and said a few words. "I just want to thank blah blah blah for their support and blah blah blah et cetera et cetera et cetera . . ." and it was while Noah was thanking everyone that Beatle noticed her—the girl sitting a few rows in front of them. Wearing her hair tied in two thick dark braids. She put her glasses on and leaned her head against her friend's and said something to her, and the friend knocked her with her arm. And Beatle was sure it was Destiny. But it couldn't be her. It was an invite-only function. Just friends of the director and producer. A bit of PR to create word of mouth. Some critics invited along as well to get some press happening.

The coincidence would be too great. And then the-girl-who-might-be-Destiny offered her friend a bite of her ice cream and Noah finished talking and the lights went down and the documentary started up. Twins upon twins upon twins, all edited neatly and talking and revealing themselves.

And the whole way through Beatle couldn't concentrate, because he kept looking over at the girl in the braids, trying to work out if it really was Destiny or not.

When the lights came back on, Beatle stayed put, waiting for the girl-who-couldn't-possibly-be-Destiny to walk past. But instead of coming back up the aisle closest to him, she went up the aisle on the far side, so he still couldn't get a handle on whether it was actually Destiny.

Beatle walked back into the foyer with Toby and Magnus and searched through the crowd for the girl-who-might-be-Destiny. He saw Nique and Harry and Charlie talking to a couple of other guys from school. His mom, Lally, and Jools were standing over by the bar. His mom was loudly saying something about ". . . my kids, up there, those last two . . ." Andrew and Tim were over near the door chatting up a couple of chicks. But there was no girl-who-might-be-Destiny.

Beatle continued scanning the crowd, *beep beep beep*, like some kind of robot, evaluating and discarding immediately anyone who didn't have long black hair tied back in braids. There weren't a whole lot of long black braids. In fact—none. Beatle couldn't see her anywhere. Surely she'd stay behind and get a drink? She wouldn't leave immediately after the screening?

Beep beep beep. Nowhere.

Beatle walked through the throng. The entire length of the lobby, around the back, down the side, looking in people's faces, to find the girl who might be Destiny. Who must have been Destiny. The girl with the long black braids.

There was the older lady whose fake blonde hair looked like it might whoosh like a bushfire if you lit a cigarette close by, and the girl whose curly hair looked like you could lie down on it and comfortably sleep for the night. There was short, straight hair and glossy dark hair, long frizzy hair, neat bobs, ponytails, pigtails, and one particular woman who had messy, crazy hair, which Beatle guessed had taken her a very long time and a lot of effort in the bathroom.

But no long black braids.

Until he spotted her. From behind. Talking to some friends over in the corner, having a lug of her drink. The closer Beatle got to her, the more he knew it was Destiny.

Definitely.

And now that he'd found her, he had to decide what to do with her.

It had been eight months—exactly, to the day—since they'd last seen each other. And the last words she'd said to him were: "I doubt I'd answer."

She'd turned away from him when he'd said he'd like to call her, and she'd scoffed as if she couldn't believe he was such a moron. "I doubt I'd answer."

There was no reason to think she'd be any happier to see him now.

But he had to go and say hi. He had to see her, talk to her, listen to that lisp thing she had going on.

He had to see whether she felt any differently towards him.

Because the way he felt about her hadn't changed since Friday the 13th of March.

He'd felt bad about breaking up with Cilla, hurting her, but he'd always known he was doing it for the right reasons. Because the only girl he wanted to be with was Destiny. Even if she wanted nothing to do with him.

He walked through the crowd towards her. A man in a suit stepped in front of him, like a warning from the universe not to go there. Beatle stopped and let the man pass, and then crossed over to where Destiny was standing with her friends and tapped her arm.

She turned around and looked up at him, a cool line settling into her mouth.

"Oh," she said, her lips looking spectacular even without a smile dancing on them. "Hi."

"Hi." He smiled. "How are you doing?"

"Fine, thanks," she said coolly. "How about you?"

"Good."

She wasn't going to make it easy for him, which was fair enough.

"I'm surprised to see you here," he said, trying to keep the conversation ticking along.

"Yes, well, probably not half as surprised as I was to see you up there on the silver screen."

And the way she said "silver screen" sounded spiky and itchy and not at all like Destiny. That lisp-thing of hers was still underlying all her words, but layered over the top was a putting-him-in-his-place type frosty icing.

The cool tone was threatening to turn to solid rock, and he noticed icicles settling on the shoulders of her friends, who were glaring at him.

"How did you like the film?" he asked.

"It was okay." She shrugged.

"Lots of interesting stories," he said and shrank to hear how lame his conversation was becoming.

"Uh-huh."

"Hmm."

He looked at her and smiled. She stared grimly back.

"You finished exams?" he asked. Okay, he was scraping the bottom of the barrel now.

"Yes."

"How'd you do?"

Destiny shrugged. "Don't know."

Beatle sighed. It seemed that no matter what he asked, she was only going to give curt answers. What was it his mom always said? No point flogging a dead horse. Something weird like that. And this here sure looked like a dead horse to him.

But he was glad he'd come over. Even if she didn't want anything to do with him. And really, what did he expect?

He'd had a girlfriend, and he had deceived them both. What kind of an asshole does something like that?

He plunged his hands into his pockets, then smiled one last time at Destiny.

"Well, I just had to come and say hi," he said. "It was nice seeing you again. I might see you around."

"Doubt it."

"Right. Well . . . bye."

"Bye," Destiny said, with a little flick of her fingers and an arched eyebrow.

And then something crashed into Beatle's head.

"Ow," he said and put his hand up to his temple.

Destiny stared at him, her eyes wide, and grabbed at his arm.

"Shit," she said. "Are you okay?"

He rubbed at his head. "Yeah, fine."

He stepped back to see what had hit him. Destiny suddenly grinned.

"God," she said, giggling, "if I didn't know better, I'd say that's a sign."

"Thought you didn't believe in signs," one of her friends said, leaning forward into their conversation.

"I don't," said Destiny, "but look." She pointed up to the ceiling. "It's a definite sign."

And again, she laughed.

It *was* a sign. That was for sure. It was a sign for that new romantic comedy that was coming out in a couple of weeks called *Cupid's Mischief.* A little cardboard cut-out of Cupid had lost one of the hooks attaching it to the ceiling, so that while the foot-end was still attached to the roof, the bow-and-arrow end was now pointing down to the ground, at exactly head height. Beatle's head-height. Beatle twisted the sign in his hands to get a good look at it.

The little plump body of Cupid was aiming a heart-tipped arrow at Beatle, a naughty sparkle in his eye and an explosion of love-hearts coming out of the arrow tip.

Beatle grinned.

He looked around the room and noticed love-hearts dangling randomly all over the joint, fluffy clouds and cherubic angels grinning from every corner. A generally loved-up feeling sprouted from the roof like flowers.

Beatle turned the sign one way, then the other. After

all these months of not believing in signs, this was one that was difficult to ignore.

"How's your head?" Destiny asked, the frost shaken off her words.

"Fine," Beatle said.

Destiny reached up and rubbed his head.

"You sure?" she asked, a softness settling into her voice.

He grinned down at her.

"Actually, now that you mention it, I am feeling a bit dizzy. Maybe if you just keep rubbing it . . ."

She grinned, and took her hand away.

"So tell me," Destiny said, looking up at him with warm, chocolatey eyes, "what were you doing in that film? I got such a shock seeing you up there."

"The director is our old art teacher."

Destiny shook her head. "No way? Mr. Castles?"

Beatle nodded.

"That's too weird," Destiny said. "He's been my art teacher this year."

That little lisp thing was gently underlying every word.

"That's freaky," Beatle agreed.

If Beatle were still the superstitious type, he'd be running through a list in his head right this moment and it would go something like this:

#1: Meeting up with Destiny again on Friday the 13th.

#2: Having Cupid donk him on his head and nearly knock him unconscious just as he was about to leave.

#3: Destiny showing up at the film in the first place—a private screening, invite only—because the director was her art teacher, too.

The list could go on. But these days Beatle was determinedly not-superstitious, so instead of writing lists in his head, he said, "Haven't seen you for a while," and looked down at her pretty face, her tasty lips.

"No," Destiny said.

Beatle picked up one of her long braids and held it in his hand.

"You're still looking as cute as I remember," he said.

"Am I?" she said, looking pleased and tilting her head. "Actually, you're a bit uglier than I remembered. Has your nose always been that big?"

Beatle grinned.

"Always. And I've definitely always been this ugly."

She grinned back.

"I'm just kidding," she said, looking down at her glass, then back up at him.

Beatle took a deep breath.

"How's your cat then?" he asked. Might as well get it over and done with. Go back to that night. "She didn't look so good last time I saw her."

"Brazilian?" Destiny asked.

"What? No, your cat. Puss, or something."

Destiny giggled.

"She was called Puss. But now we call her Brazilian. Is that cruel? To change your cat's name when she's four years old? But when your cat arrives home one night completely shaved, you really have no option but to change her name."

Beatle blurted out a laugh.

"Does everyone call her Brazilian?" he asked.

"Oh sure, Mum, Dad, everyone."

And she tilted her head at him and grinned.

"So how is Brazilian?" he asked.

Destiny raised an eyebrow.

"And how's your cat?" he added.

She laughed and smacked his shoulder.

"Fine. Thanks for asking."

And they stood looking at each other.

"Hey, I'm really sorry about everything," he said, holding onto her hand. "It was fucked."

"It was pretty fucked," she agreed.

He looked down at the carpet.

"You never called," she said.

"You wouldn't have answered."

"True," she said. "But that shouldn't have stopped you from trying."

Beatle lifted his eyes from the carpet to look at her.

"You wanted me to call?" he asked.

"No way," she said. "Definitely not. And if you had, I would have told you not to call me again." Her look softened. "But that doesn't mean you shouldn't have tried."

Beatle frowned.

Maybe, after all, it was easier to do things according to random signs scattered around the universe, to consult horoscopes, to not step on cracks. It would have made as much sense as what Destiny was saying to him.

"So you wanted me to call?" he asked once more.

"No. Definitely not. But I sort of expected you'd give it a try."

Beatle grinned.

"What if I called now?" he asked, trying to see past her eyes, trying to see into where her thoughts were hidden. "Now that we've caught up again? Would you speak to me, or tell me not to bother you?"

She shrugged. "Not sure. Hard to tell."

Figuring he might as well find out sooner than later, Beatle pulled out his phone, right there in the lobby, found her number, and pushed the green button. From her handbag a ringing sounded. She looked at him without moving. Beatle stood there with his phone against his ear, feeling his face go red. He had meant it to be a joke, not a mass humiliation, but that's how it was turning out.

He could see her friends standing close by, watching his face, listening as her phone rang inside her bag.

And then, just as Beatle was about to flip his phone shut, she reached inside her bag and took hers out.

"Hello?" she said, turning slightly away from him.

"Destiny," he said.

"Who's calling please?" she asked.

He grinned. "Beatle."

She glanced at him. "Beatle who?"

He grinned.

"What are you doing?" he asked.

"At this film thing. How about you?"

"Nothing much."

He looked at her.

"You wanna go get an ice cream?" he said into his phone. "I'd really like to see you again."

"An ice cream?" she said. "Déjà vu."

"No. Chocolate."

She laughed. "I don't like chocolate," she said.

"How about vanilla?" Beatle asked.

"Well, I'm not sure," she said, lowering her voice. "Last time I met you, you were a flesh-eating psychopath with an appetite for vestal virgins, and a girlfriend on the side. Anything changed, or is it the same old same old?"

Beatle stepped closer, still talking into his phone, but looking into her face.

"No girlfriend. No flesh-eating. No vestal virgins. And did I mention there's definitely no girlfriend?"

"Well, in that case," she said, shutting her phone, "I suppose I could fit you into my busy schedule."

She looked up at him. He looked down at her and pushed a strand of hair behind her ear, gently, so that there was nothing obscuring her beautiful face.

She introduced Beatle to her friends. Toby and Magnus drifted over and met Destiny, Netta, and Mathilde.

Even though he hadn't seen her for eight months, it seemed to Beatle like it was just yesterday they'd been sitting next to each other, spooning crazily named ice cream into their mouths.

"You wanna split this joint?" Beatle asked.

"I can't leave my friends," Destiny said.

"They should come," Beatle told her.

After all, the sooner he got to know them, the better.

As the six of them walked outside, other filmgoers closed the gap behind them in the lobby. Occasionally someone or other got donked on the head by Cupid's arrow, and laughed, saying it's "a definite sign," that "it had to mean something." One guy grabbed his girlfriend and lifted her up so that she was hit on the head by the arrow and then declared, "There, now you've got no choice but to fall in love with me," and she laughed as he put her back down on the ground and kissed her mouth.

Love-hearts dangled from the ceiling and plump cherubs watched as Beatle and Destiny walked down the stairs of the theater, followed by their friends.

And if you were even slightly the superstitious type, you might think to yourself that those two were made for each other.

THE END
(EVER AFTER)

A Note from the Author

Melbourne, Australia, (pronounced *Mel-bn*) is not to be confused with Melbourne, Florida. It's the second-largest city in Australia and has about 4.5 million people, no hurricanes, and no alligators.

Yes, Melbourne is a long way away from the USA, but we have a lot in common. We have cool kids and not so cool kids, same as in every US city. Here we call uncool kids *dags*, one of our many slang words. (http://www.aussieslang.com/)

East St Kilda—where Beatle lives—is a hip suburb that has an edge because it's full of cool *funsters* (musicians, artists, and filmmakers) living side by side with a huge migrant community that has settled here from all over the world. It's pronounced East Saint Kilda but never spelled that way. Always East St Kilda. Some tourists call it East *Street* Kilda when they first arrive, because that's how it looks, but are fairly quickly alerted to their mistake by the locals hooting with laughter. (http://en.wikipedia.org/wiki/St_Kilda_East,_Victoria)

The tram stop where Beatle and Destiny first meet is out front of the Espy (http://www.espy.com.au/), a grungy pub (hotel) in St Kilda that bestows instant cred on anyone who goes there. If you want to see a band, you go to the Espy. If you want to see a stand-up comic, you go to the Espy. If you don't want to see your parents, you go to the Espy. It's a Melbourne institution kind of like CBGBs (http://www.cbgb.com/history1.htm) was in New York.

Kew—where Destiny lives—is full of expensive things: expensive houses, expensive schools, expensive cars, expensive hair, expensive teeth. It's like a town in

Connecticut, except it's a suburb in Melbourne. A cool teenager living in Kew would spend a fair chunk of time on the No. 16 tram rattling across the city to hip East St Kilda.

Trams

Melbourne is famous for them and you can travel in them all over the city.
(http://en.wikipedia.org/wiki/Melbourne_trams)

Some cities in the USA, including Memphis, Seattle, and San Francisco, have bought old trams from Melbourne and now use them as tourist trams.

School Year

In Melbourne, the school year starts in February and goes until the beginning of December. So while the Alice

Cooper classic "School's Out for Summer" is raucously sung on the last day of each school year, Melbourne kids sing it in December instead of June.

Drinking and Driving

In Melbourne, once you turn eighteen you can do everything you want, pretty much. You can drink, you can drive (although not at the same time, of course), and you can party like it's 1999 (or 2999). Eighteen is the big milestone for Melbourne kids.

Thanx

Jenny Darling and Donica Bettanin for backing me and taking the manuscript to a whole new level. Cat McCredie for sweating the small stuff, editing up a storm, and making a huge difference. Laura Harris for believing in a little book called *Beatle Meets Destiny*. Robin Benjamin for hauling this story from down under to the US of A and the biggest audience in the world. Kristin Gill, Anyez Lindop, and Rose Jost for blitzing it in the real world. Andrew McAliece and Meg McMena for being outstanding workshop buddies. Dominique, Harry, and Andrew for reading early drafts—over and over again. Rachel Skinner for suggesting I write for a young adult audience. Tom Pearce for skateboarding lingo. Matt Conron for helping me stretch the limits of medical believability. Mum for a new computer when the old one packed in. India Robinson, Eliza and Holly Lambert, Dominique, Harry, and Charlie for giving straight-up feedback on the cover. Dominique, Harry, and Charlie for letting me write, even when they wanted me to do something else. Andrew. For making each and every day a lucky one.